KNOCKOUT

BENSON FIRST RESPONDERS
BOOK 5

LISA PHILLIPS

TWO DOGS PUBLISHING, LLC.

eBook ISBN: 979-8-88552-176-5

Paperback ISBN: 979-8-88552-177-2

Published by Two Dogs Publishing, LLC. Idaho, USA

Cover Design by Sasha Almazan and Gene Mollica, GS Cover Design Studio, LLC

Edited by Christy Callahan, Professional Publishing Services

Audiobook published by Recorded Books

ONE

T EN YEARS AGO

Officer Roger O'Connell pulled the radio car to
the curb outside the Quick Sip. His partner, the rookie he'd
been tasked with training, Officer Davey Turnbull, shifted in
his seat. Nervous.

"Let's go." Roger shoved his door open. "Stay behind me."

Try not to shoot me in the back. Roger flipped off the siren
but left the lights flashing. He slammed the car door and
immediately heard a scream.

He pulled his duty weapon from its holster and pushed
the door to the gas station open. "Benson Police Department!"

"Go away!"

Roger followed the voice to the far side of the Quick Sip.
The call had come in for a man with a gun. No shots fired,
possibly mentally unstable. Those were the calls Roger always
had prioritized to him—since he'd started to see a pattern in

street patrols. He'd been doing this long enough that he could call in favors, do some digging on his own.

If he found evidence of something, he would kick it upstairs. Until then, he kept his eyes open.

Something was going on in Benson.

No one at the Veterans Affairs medical center or the local hospital could answer his questions. They didn't seem to be aware of a rash of older men who should be on medication, or even in treatment programs, that were out on the streets instead and not in those programs. He'd dug quietly so far, putting together suspicion until he was ready with the evidence to present an actual case.

Would this be the missing piece he needed?

Discovering the connection in these cases wouldn't help him figure out how to get his son Liam to call him from deployment, or how to get his younger boys, Conrad and Rory, to clean their room. But it would be a step in the right direction for Benson. A way to make the world his boys lived in a better place.

Officer Turnbull said, "I'll go right."

Roger glanced over once at the guy's retreating form. He might not make it as a cop if he didn't get a handle on those nerves.

A couple of people crouched at the end of the aisle. Roger said, "Get them out." Then he headed for whoever had answered his callout. "I'm Officer O'Connell. I'm here to help."

He stepped past the Pringles all lined up on the shelf and peered at the front register. An employee hunkered behind the desk, wide-eyed. Young, maybe early twenties, the guy had greasy hair and a salmon-colored T-shirt. The way he stared, he probably wanted a show of force. Roger's tactic was *not* to come in with guns blazing and save the day. This young man might want Roger to shoot first and then start with the follow-up questions, but so much of policing was about going slow, looking for ways to defuse a situation until there was no other choice but to use force.

"Sir?"

The man in front of the counter swung around. He had a Glock in one hand and wore only plain white boxers with tube socks and black slides. Long hair to his shoulders flew everywhere and matched his wild eyes.

Roger held his gun angled down. "How's it going?"

He always went for defusing first. Never escalation.

Hopefully, Officer Turnbull was currently getting people out of the Quick Sip to safety. The kid wanted to be a hero, so that should suit him just fine.

Kind of reminded Roger of his son Liam, all wild and determined to save the world. So much determination and strength. It made him proud even if his oldest didn't want to be a cop. No, he'd rather traipse around the world with his Marine buddies.

"I'm Roger." He lifted his chin. "What's your name?"

The guy thought for a second. His mouth worked. Finally he said, "Will."

"All right. It's nice to meet you, Will." Roger scanned the tattoos that covered most of the man's exposed skin. "Marines?"

Will nodded.

"My son is a marine." Roger gave his battalion and company numbers.

Will seemed confused about how to respond.

"I have a problem here, Will." Roger took a step toward him. "I need you to hand over that gun you have. There's a lot of scared people in here. I think you and I make them nervous."

Will looked down at his hand, seemingly surprised he had a gun.

"They just want to go about their day." Roger paused. "How about you give me the gun, and we let them get back to their lives?" Roger took another half step. "We can get some coffee. Talk."

"What is there to talk about?" Every muscle in Will's torso stood out, evidence of his tension. "You think you can help me?"

"I can certainly try." Roger let that sink in. "You gonna let me do that?"

Will eyed him.

"I need your help. So these people can stop being scared."

"That won't happen." A defensive look crept into Will's expression.

He thought there was something worth being scared about? Something regular folk should be concerned by... which could be anything. "Even still." Roger held out one hand and motioned with his fingers. "I need you to give me that gun."

The young guy behind the counter ducked out of sight. Roger didn't blame him. There were at least six people in here and more who had run outside. Was anyone hurt?

He needed to contain the assailant so he could find out. The difference between a successful resolution and a tragic catastrophe often rested on a knife-edge, ready to tip one way or the other in a split second. What he did next could mean the difference between life and death for the people in here— or himself and his partner, or the assailant.

"Will, can you tell me what there is to be scared about?"

Will stared at him. "Can't get no help. Can't get no freedom."

"From who?"

"Those commies still takin' everythin'. Can't get no help."

"I'll help you." Roger took another step, still several feet back. "Give me the gun."

Will glanced to the side, down the aisle. "You're a liar. You're not gonna help."

"I am, but you have to trust me. I'm not going to let you down." Roger needed him to hand over the weapon, so he said again, "No one is going to hurt you. We're only here to help."

Will kept staring behind him. Roger started to turn. To see if Officer Turnbull stood there.

Will said, "You're not going to help. You're one of them, sent to take me out."

A gun went off. The guy behind the counter screamed.

Officer Turnbull had fired. Roger twisted back around to see what had happened to the employee. Will shoved at him, and they both started to fall. Pain exploded in Roger's back. He hit the floor, and the world swam around him.

Another shot. He hadn't recognized there had been another shot.

Not until it was too late.

TWO

PRESENT DAY

A SECOND BEFORE THE ELEVATOR DOORS SLID CLOSED, A manicured hand waved between, and they retracted. Roxanne sighed. Maybe next time she would make the ride up to the Cold Cases floor of Vanguard Private Security alone, but not this morning.

She lifted her coffee cup to her lips and smiled politely as a prim young woman stepped in. Tight skirt and blouse, a light jacket, and designer purse. She eyed Roxanne and blinked, barely stifling the reaction.

Yeah, you look great, too. Roxanne had been a marine for years, and she'd never quite let go of having her hair tied back—today it was in two braids. She'd also never quite let go of carrying a pack or wearing pants with pockets that could actually hold things. Functional trumped stylish any day, even if she looked like a casually dressed operator rather than someone who worked in a corporate office.

If she came in wearing a skirt and heels, the guys in Cold Cases would have heart attacks. She preferred to save those outfits for undercover work. At night. On street corners.

Otherwise, it was flats and clothes she could fight in because it wasn't worth getting caught off guard and leaving herself vulnerable.

Again.

Ms. Prim and Proper looked down her nose, then jabbed the button for the main office. "Good morning."

"Hey." Roxie took another sip of her coffee.

Ms. Prim and Proper eyed Roxie one more time. Couldn't help it. Needed to get an up-close look.

Take it in, you get one shot.

Roxie tensed her arm to fight the need to brush hair in front of her ear to cover the scar on the side of her face that stretched from her part down her hairline to her ear.

One shot.

It was what she'd given Mark. Now it was her turn.

The other woman smiled. "I'm Lena, by the way."

Ah. She nodded. "Roxanne. Cold Cases." So, this was Lena. It made sense now that she got a look at the woman— which might sound harsh, but she'd heard the story.

"I'm Clare's assistant."

Roxie nearly said, "Good for you."

Peter Olson, a young guy she worked with in Cold Cases, had told her all about how Lena two-timed him and his twin brother, Simon, who worked in tech. She'd dated both, strung them along, and caused the twins to be at odds. Simon was still affected by it, while Peter had fallen for a young woman on an operation over the summer. He and Selena had survived a hijacked cruise ship, and now they were dating.

The guy even had a picture of her on his desk.

Roxanne's summer had been less high risk, training with a search and rescue school that taught dog handling. She'd left that career path behind for reasons that were best unsaid. Sure, she'd gotten certified, but she hadn't chosen a dog—though, she was on their "call" list in case they needed additional help for anything.

Tessa, the trainer she'd worked with, had texted to check in, but Roxanne hadn't called back. After what happened with River and Tessa, and their dogs, she just couldn't pretend everything was fine.

When the doors opened on Roxie's floor, she offered a "Have a good day" over her shoulder and headed for Cold Cases.

Not many employees ventured onto this floor. Most worked out of the main office where Clare—the Vanguard CEO—could be a part of the day-to-day work. This floor took a more "boots on the ground" approach to their work.

Locker room. Break room. A small gym, separate from the training gym upstairs that had its own floor. They had a bullpen with banks of computers. Whiteboard walls they could brainstorm all over when they needed to figure out where to find a lead, and other walls covered with open cases and success stories. Like the west wall, which now had a picture of local PD Officer River Gaines under a sign that said SOLVED.

Peter was the one who had solved that, figuring out the identity of the cop who had been found as a child with no idea who he was and no parents. Since Roxie had met him and was friends with the woman River had fallen for—Tessa, the search and rescue trainer—the case had thankfully been put to rest.

She sipped her coffee and headed for her desk in an

alcove because that was the spot she had chosen where she could see all the exits.

Roxie fired up her computer. No new emails in response to her inquiries about the case she was really here to solve—the missing woman she was trying to locate. Even though the lady was likely already dead, answers were still out there.

Then she would have what she needed to move on with her life.

"Meeting in five!" Bob Davis spoke so fast, calling out across the office, that he'd ducked back into his office before she ever saw his face. Just a blur at the corner of her vision.

She locked her computer so no one could access her profile without her password.

The screen darkened, and she stared at the outline of her own reflection. She couldn't see the scars, the years of military shadow in her eyes, or the pain of so many mistakes. If her parents were still alive, they would be ashamed of her. Most of the time, she tried not to be ashamed of herself, though it was hard.

Then there was a certain SWAT sergeant who made her time in the marines predominantly fond memories of time spent with him. And yet now those were the worst of all her memories when coupled with what might have been. *Never would be now* was a kind of sweet torture.

Probably a pointless dream, anyway.

What was the use of worrying about something that never was when she had something more pressing to take care of?

Roxie pushed away all those distractions. She needed to be mission focused, like the single-minded days of deployment with her unit in Kandahar. Distractions got you killed—something she'd learned the hard way. Even praying God would save her hadn't worked. She'd made her own way out, struggled and bled, and finally crawled to safety.

She left her coffee and headed for the briefing room, which had a huge conference table and nine chairs.

Six were occupied. Bob Davis, the department chair, was a former cop who had served a prison sentence for charges related to police corruption. He'd done his time and was now elbow deep in his second chance at making the world a better place.

Peter, twenty-three or twenty-four, had been hired by Clare, along with his twin, as an alternative to serving a sentence for hacking. The other four, she hadn't met more than to say hi in the week since she had been officially brought on as an employee.

"Have a seat." Bob motioned to Peter, who hit a button on his laptop, which was connected to the screen on the wall. "This week's highlight is a ten-year-old case. I'll walk you through it in a second, but I'm going to assign it to Roxanne to tackle. Good way to get your feet wet, and I'll be around to assist if needed. Though, for the most part, you'll just read through the files and follow up with the officers to start with. Talk to whoever you can."

Roxie nodded. Everyone else had a case, but she was new. Bob liked to walk them through investigations, mostly what private citizens brought to them, because the police didn't have the time or resources to look into cold cases. Bob had connections in the prosecutor's office and the PD, though most of them didn't much want to talk with a former dirty cop even if he had served his time.

Peter's connection ran a little stronger, with his sister now married to a Benson PD detective.

Roxanne hadn't even mentioned her personal connection to the SWAT sergeant. She didn't plan to bring it up. Ever.

On the screen behind Bob, a photo came up—then another right beside it. Both were of the same man. In one, he was wearing a military uniform and very much alive. The other was a picture from the morgue.

"He was a marine?" She sat up straighter in her chair.

Some cases were never solved, tragically. Some missing people didn't want to be found, or circumstances meant they couldn't be. Roxanne wasn't going to let that stop her from getting answers.

She stared at the marine's picture. Was that the reason Bob had assigned it to her, because they shared a commonality?

Bob said, "His death was ten years ago. He was receiving treatment at a private clinic that works with the VA. Earlier that week, he had an altercation with the police, and one officer was killed during that. But the dead guy was found three days later in an alley. Reported as an overdose, but I'm not sure I buy it. There are marks indicating he was restrained."

Roxie frowned. "He wasn't arrested after killing the cop?"

One of her coworkers sitting on her left flipped a page in the paper file in front of him. "Looks like he ran off in the confusion. Got away. The partner tried to save the officer's life."

Peter said, "The deceased officer is the father of a friend of mine, so I'd like to help figure out what happened."

Roxie nodded. "We could work it together."

Bob rapped his knuckles on the table. "Fine by me. I'd like to find out if someone murdered the cop killer."

When he put it like that, it almost sounded like a nonstarter. Wouldn't killing the man responsible for a cop's death be a good thing? Might be that the police department didn't want this stone overturned. Perhaps one of their officers had cleaned up the situation and never reported that they got revenge.

Not exactly procedure.

She'd have to ask Peter about that later. But for now, she said, "Why do we believe it was murder rather than simply accidental? Didn't you say overdose?"

Bob worked his mouth around. "Call it a hunch." He wrapped his knuckles on the table again. "Everyone else has cases to work, so let's go around, and you can tell me where you're at."

The guy to her left closed the file. Roxie pulled it over to her, so she could hang on to it. While they talked, she flipped open the case.

Halfway down the page, she spotted the name of the deceased police officer.

Roger O'Connell.

Roxie winced. She couldn't work this case. Not if she had to talk to Liam, which she would have to in order to explore all possible leads.

Why couldn't she catch a break just once in her life?

THREE

L iam O'Connell pressed down on the gas pedal, both hands grasping the wheel. Lights and sirens going. It was quiet in the passenger seat, where Officer Blake Reed sat, and in the back, where he had Officer Jasper Hollingsworth and two guys from patrol they'd been training a few months now so they could be on-call SWAT officers rather than full-time.

The SUV in front of them kept going the same way they were, completely ignoring the lights and sirens Liam had on.

"Oh no." Liam moved forward in his seat.

Someone in the back said, "Told you," in a low voice. "He always knows when something is about to go down. Before it even happens."

Liam ignored the comment and kept his focus on the gray SUV. The driver swerved to the curb, sideswiped a parked car, and came to a stop at an angle with one tire on the curb. The car's position completely nixed Liam's ability to see the driver's door. To approach he'd have to get out and expose himself to weapons fire.

"Get me eyes on the car."

Jasper grabbed his handle. "On it."

The guy operated their drone, which would give Liam eyes inside, even thermal imaging. They needed to know if there was more than the driver inside.

He cracked his door. The others climbed out and got into position behind him.

Liam approached the back corner of the car and called out, "Morgan Alakov, get out of the car with your hands up. You are under arrest."

A slew of accented expletives came as the suspect's answer.

Liam had his rifle ready and the paperwork in his pocket. "We have a warrant for your arrest. Exit the vehicle slowly with your hands where I can see them."

Cars driving past slowed to watch. Someone from the cafe and the laundromat next to it came to their windows. Liam tuned it all out. The patrol officers on the team had been trained to push back on civilians getting too close. He needed to know the Russian wasn't going to fire on anyone.

He used a lower tone to say, "Hollingsworth, where's my drone?"

"Deploying now." The whiz of the drone followed Jasper's comment.

The drone flew over their vehicle, then over the SUV where it hovered above the hood.

Jasper said, "I've got someone in the back seat."

"Copy that." Liam took a step, exposing himself on the left side of the car, in an effort to draw the suspect's attention. "Morgan Alakov, get out of the car with your hands in view. We have a warrant for your arrest." To his teammates, he said, "Get them out on the right side."

Blake would be first on that, guiding the other officers to

the rear door on the right in order to extract the second person —whether they were an accomplice or an innocent. Either way, they would get a shot at getting out of this.

"Morgan Alakov, open the door and step out." Liam watched the door and the surroundings. "Comply or we will use force." It was better if the suspect opened the door himself. Ideally, Alakov would come to Liam peacefully and surrender himself to be arrested.

"What are you doing?" the suspect yelled. "What's that drone doing? I don't wanna get scanned. That thing is scanning me! It's infringing on my rights!"

"We have a warrant for your arrest. Get out of the car slowly with your hands up." In a lower voice, for the benefit of the officers they were training, he said, "I could do this all day."

Someone's chuckle came back to him across the radio channel.

Morale was good. But not for much longer. He needed to tell Officer Blake Reed and Officer Jasper Hollingsworth that their SWAT team was being disbanded thanks to budget cuts. Their team was being moved from full-time to a collateral team—officers who worked within other departments and were on call for SWAT.

He'd need to get Jasper and Blake settled with other squads and find a position for himself as a sergeant.

What department would be a good fit? There were no open spots in intelligence. Jasper and Blake could take the detective exam and build their futures. He could go back to patrol or work in training. He had options.

Things would be different in the future, no matter how he felt about change. It wasn't his strong suit—and he knew he should pray through it. Life didn't come with a guarantee, or a manual. But like the PD, it came with best practices, standards to adhere to, and ways they could ensure things turned out the best they could—at least as far as it was in his power to accomplish.

The engine of the Russian's vehicle revved. He couldn't let this guy run again.

"Drone on the tires, Jas." He had an official way of saying it, but they'd been working together long enough they had their own shorthand. A few seconds later, he heard one tire hiss out air, and then the drone flew around the back of the SUV.

"What is that alien thing doing? Get it out of here!" Alakov yelled.

The drone poked out all the tires, so the suspect couldn't drive away. Liam could also shoot out the wing mirrors, but if he could distract the driver, then Blake could get the second person out.

Liam said, "Move in."

Lord, guide my steps here. My words.

He took a step since being visible to the driver meant he wasn't looking at the passenger side—where Blake headed for the rear door—and repeated his command.

The rear door could be locked or unlocked.

Lord, help us.

He took another step. "You're under arrest."

"Approaching the passenger side." The notification came from Blake through his headphones.

Liam stepped out wide so he'd be able to see in the window. The suspect was low-level and Russian-connected. The brother of a guy they'd brought in months ago, who had lawyered up and refused to talk.

Now they needed to talk to Morgan. The arrest warrant was for multiple counts of domestic battery as well as possession with intent to sell. He'd evaded custody so far, but if they got him in an interrogation room they could flip him with a deal to give them information on the Russians above him in the hierarchy.

They needed to take down the whole organization. That would start with finding probable cause for a search warrant. Getting into the organization's financials. Their business practices.

It was the only way to prove it was Nico Obolensky's brother, Raphi, who had set the bomb that took out the old man, their uncle, a few months ago. He wanted to find the men who were accomplices in the shooting of Benson PD Officer River Gaines, and the injury of his dog. Both had retired since then. Liam owed it to them to work this case.

Underlying that motivation were the Russians' dealings with his own family. The fact he and Raphi had been duking it out since Liam joined the force six years ago—following in his father's footsteps. They'd dogged his dad's steps through his career.

"Step out of the car!" Liam took another step, gaining ground. The suspect could pull a weapon, shoot at them. He was looking around, thinking. Trying to come up with a way out of this. "Hands where I can see them."

The suspect raised his hands above the ledge so Liam could see his fingers.

"It's over. Get out." Liam held his weapon ready but not pointed at the suspect. He wasn't going to shoot the guy. He'd rather use the stun gun on his belt first if force was necessary.

He unsnapped the clip but didn't slide the stun gun out.

A woman yelped. The suspect started to yell. Liam shouted again for compliance.

"Got her." That was Blake.

"Hey, what are you doing?" The suspect, still in the front seat of the car, now started to climb toward the back.

Liam directed the second officer to open the door, then he grabbed the suspect's shirt and dragged him out of the car. "You're under arrest."

"Get off me! Karina, you keep your mouth shut. Don't tell them anything!" He struggled against Liam's grasp on his elbow.

"Hands above your head." The name Karina threw him, but he couldn't dive into that abyss right now. He had to focus.

The suspect's raised hands gave Liam a clear look at the man's belt, clear of a weapon tucked there. Liam backed up, as did the officer behind him. "Turn around slowly. Keep your hands above your head."

Blake came around the back of the car. "Sarge, switch out."

Liam frowned. He didn't ask questions, knowing the only reason Blake would ask to trade places was if the innocent were secure and there was a good reason.

Karina.

Veronika's sister.

Veronika had been his confidential informant with the Russians up until a few months ago when she was killed for it. He'd left Karina alone after that, unable to face her. He'd met them early on in his rookie days when they'd been in high school. Now they were early twenties, and he'd had to watch Karina bury her sister.

Because of him.

Blake took up Liam's position, so he rounded the back of the car and headed to where the woman sat on the curb. One SWAT officer watched over her, and Jasper wasn't far away since he'd landed the drone.

She looked up, and Liam's heart sank. "Karina." What

was she doing with the Russians? He crouched in front of her. "You wanna tell me why you're riding shotgun on my arrest?"

She blinked, and her eyes filled with tears. "Liam." Those tears rolled down her face. "I think I need help."

No kidding.

And she wasn't the only one.

FOUR

Roxie scrolled down on her computer screen so she could keep reading. The police report on the homeless veteran's death was pretty sparse. William Lincoln Turner had died alone in an alley, by all accounts. No one had collected much in terms of evidence. An autopsy hadn't been done, just a drug test that had come back positive for a cocktail of uppers and downers that would prolong a high—and in this case, had contained a lethal dose for this man. Something new to him, or his heart hadn't been able to take the strain anymore.

No dealer killed their client on purpose. That didn't make sense.

Drugs were manufactured to make the most money, stretching the purity with other substances that could have nasty effects.

A mug of coffee landed beside her hand.

Roxie flinched and twisted around, trying not to flip out of her skin at being jogged from her thoughts.

"Sorry." Peter grabbed a chair and slid it over to sit by her.

"Don't worry about it." The guy was a good kid, who

might be a trained operative now, but he still made her feel every one of the years of experience she had on him. She was about to turn thirty-one. Nearly ten years older than him, and sometimes it felt like a hundred.

"What have you found so far?"

"I'm still familiarizing myself with the victim." She hadn't yet gotten to the incident involving Liam's father. "He has a niece who lives in Seattle still, but she's never lived here and only spoke with officers over the phone when they informed her of his death as his next of kin."

Peter sipped from his own coffee.

"Maybe he has friends from the Corps." She still had contacts in the military. Perhaps one of them could give her information on his teammates or his squad. Marines that he would've kept in contact with. Everyone she knew and had been friends with from the Marines, she'd cut them out of her life afterward.

Shame. Necessity.

Didn't matter which it was. She'd had to build back friendships and got to choose who she had in her life right now. Her roommate was her best friend. Things were easy there. Why complicate it?

"Good idea," Peter said. "Maybe Liam can give us some context on the incident with his father. A cop's point of view."

"He was still in when it happened." They had been deployed when his father was killed in the line of duty. She tried not to let on that talking about him wasn't easy.

"I'll see if he can meet us. Maybe for lunch."

She looked at her screen. "There's a lot to read through. Why don't you do lunch and catch me up when you're back?"

Peter said nothing.

Roxie glanced over to see how much she'd managed to

fool him. *Not much, by the look of his expression.* "Dividing tasks gets them done faster."

"Mmm." Peter took a sip, staring at her over the rim of the mug. "Right."

Roxie slumped back into the chair. "Fine. Ask."

"I heard you two had...words."

Roxie sighed. "During the search for River's father?"

"They said you and Liam were off to the side, having some kind of heated discussion."

"I really don't want to talk about it." She winced.

Peter frowned. "Did he hurt you?"

Yes, but not the way you think. Liam thought she'd hurt him with no regard for his feelings, so he'd lashed out. Hurt her instead. "Both of us said things we regret." Hopefully, he regretted it as much as she did. Otherwise, her opinion of him had been all wrong, and he wasn't a good man.

She couldn't have that bad of judgment, could she?

Roxie sighed. "It doesn't matter, anyway."

"Maybe it's you that needs to go to lunch," Peter suggested. "Clear the air on some things."

At least he didn't suggest they were going to kiss and make up. "It's not that simple." She wasn't in a place in her life where she could "figure things out" with a guy. Wouldn't lead to anything, so what was the point? Even if her roommate was a hopeless romantic. "Can we just leave the Liam thing alone?"

Peter's expression softened. "We can."

Great, now he thought she needed sympathy. She was about to clear the air on that—without telling him why she'd come to Benson in the first place, even though it wasn't like she had a home anywhere else—when thankfully, Peter's twin brother, Simon, strolled around the corner into the bullpen.

No need to dig a hole with all the things she didn't want to say.

The twins were identical but very different. When he'd become an operator, Peter had cut his hair short in a military style, though it was longer on top. Simon left his long, so it hung down over his ears, and he ran his hands back through it when he needed to think something over. Peter had gained some muscle through training, but both were lean and five-foot-eleven at least. In comparison, Liam was like a redwood tree.

She didn't usually feel short at five-foot-seven, but with these two, it happened. She lifted her mug toward the approaching twin. "Want some?"

"I've had two cans of Celsius already." Simon grinned as he approached the side of her desk. "I'll be awake until Wednesday."

She chuckled. "Do you need to be?" Maybe he was tech support on a multi-day operation that would last until midweek.

"Probably not." He lifted his shoulder in a kind of shrug, which Peter returned. Some twin greeting only they knew the meaning of. "I ran the guy you're working. Looked for similar cases where a veteran was reported deceased. Tried to find any connection I could to another case."

Roxie frowned. "If it wasn't murder, because he really did just overdose, why would there be a pattern of kills?" She'd done a ton of research into murder investigation, and Clare—who ran Vanguard—had sent her on several training courses. She glanced at Peter. Why be in denial, except that she'd rather believe someone connected to Liam's father hadn't been murdered? "You really think the death was suspicious?"

"I think every death is suspicious. It's not natural, and it won't ever be. Even if it's peaceful."

His attitude made sense since they'd lost their parents, and almost lost their sister. To Simon, she said, "What did you find?"

He waved her back from her computer and pressed a series of keys so fast she couldn't keep up. Peter had the same level of skill with tech, but he wanted a different career path than his brother. She didn't blame him. A fresh start sounded great.

Simon pulled up a series of files in a folder. "Each one of these is an overdose or accidental death of a veteran in the last fifteen years. Four decedents, each one with the same cocktail of drugs, though there are a few minor differences."

"So they had the same dealer."

"Maybe." Simon clicked the mouse, and a bunch of crime scene photos of the victims popped up. "On the surface, they're tragic deaths of people who should have been better served by the government they sacrificed for. Dig a little, and we start to see correlations."

She glanced at Peter. "Did you get him working this?"

He nodded. "Looks to me like there's some similarity in the positioning even. Someone being careful. What about clean up?"

Simon said, "Distinct lack of evidence. Needle marks but no needles. No IDs or money, so it could look like a robbery gone wrong." He shrugged. "That's for you guys to figure out."

Roxie scrunched up her nose. "I'm not sure." There might not be enough here to show they were connected. "Why does Bob want us to look into this in the first place? That would help us get a clue where to go with it."

Peter said, "Maybe he doesn't want to pollute our ideas by giving us a direction to go. Or maybe they don't want anyone to know they asked us to take a look."

"What else connects them other than their chosen career and the fact they were set adrift after?" The speculation was interesting but didn't prove anything. They needed to dig more before she would believe there was something more than just tragedy here. "Support groups. Programs. Anything at all that indicates they were targeted, or why?"

"I'll find out." Simon straightened. "I'm still working, but I wanted to bring you this."

"I'll run with it. Thanks." He'd probably wanted to come to this floor and see his brother. Then there was Bob, who might want to take down a local dealer as a favor for a friend.

But the fact there were this many deaths over so many years?

Something might be going on.

FIVE

"Thanks." Liam waited for Karina to slide into the booth, and then he did the same opposite her.

The server nodded, not quite sure of him—probably his size since she was petite. Her gaze scanned the emblem on his black T-shirt and the badge on his belt, along with everything else he had clipped there. Finally, she walked away.

He spotted Blake and Jasper, who had gone right to a two-top at the bar so they could get waited on by Blake's sister. They'd processed Morgan Alakov through to holding, so he could get transferred to the county jail and walked Karina through her statement. After he'd written up his report, he'd suggested lunch. Mainly to check in with this woman.

At the station across the street, he'd grilled her on the reason she'd been in that car this morning. Now that they were at Backdraft Bar and Grill, the franchise Liam's brother ran here in Benson, he needed to ask her not just why, but dig and figure out where her head was at since her sister's death.

He left the menu alone because he could practically recite

it at this point. "I figured you'd be at your new job since it's a Monday."

She didn't meet his gaze, just stared at the menu in her hands. "It didn't work out. I'm looking again."

And meanwhile, making poor choices about who to spend time with. "How'd you really meet Alakov?"

Liam and his team had arrested Morgan's brother, Sergei Alakov, a few months ago, but the guy had lawyered up right away and said nothing about who he worked for.

Then another man with ties to the Russians had been killed in the police station a few days later.

Since then, everyone they brought in refused to talk even though the likelihood of it happening again wasn't high. Nico Obolensky had stolen a uniform, snuck in, and killed the guy they had in custody. But he'd met his end in death. His brother Raphi was the real problem at this point.

"Do you know Raphi Obolensky?"

"I thought this was lunch, not work." She ran a finger down the menu. "I think I'll have chicken Caesar salad."

Liam said, "It's not about work."

"But you're gonna use me to get information." She let go of the menu, and it flopped to the table. "Like my sister?"

Liam pressed his lips together.

"I know what happened to Veronika wasn't your fault. But she was working for you."

"She only told me what she wanted to. I never asked her to put herself in danger." Out of the corner of his eye, Liam spotted his brother, Conrad, exiting the kitchen, looking for him. He lifted one finger so his younger brother held off. "You know how sorry I am that someone took her life."

"They left her in a pool of blood in her living room."

Liam had been there through the investigation and evidence collection, and then he helped follow up on leads in the weeks after. A lot of the lab results were still out, but as far as the detective was concerned, the case may as well be cold.

It had been stuffed into a drawer with a calendar notification on the detective's computer to look over the case once a month until it got even colder. Then it would switch to every few months or even a year out. All in the hopes that revisiting everything would jog something loose.

Was the detective not convinced the results would yield a lead, or had he been coerced into giving it minimal effort?

Liam swallowed. "I'll follow up with the lab again, see if they will have results on anything soon."

Karina shifted in her seat.

Liam caught a note of nervousness. Where had that come from? Maybe she was protecting her boyfriend. Had Morgan Alakov murdered Veronika? Of course, Karina might not be spending time with him if that were the case, but he'd seen stranger things in his career.

The server took their order. He told her to tell his brother that he'd come find him after he'd eaten. Right now, he needed to dig a little more with Karina.

"How'd you get hooked up with Morgan?" She'd told them in her statement that she'd only met him recently and he had been driving her home after they spent the night together. Not good, considering Alakov's connection to dangerous criminals. "He's not a nice guy."

Liam couldn't tell her the information contained within the warrant or what he knew about Morgan's criminal history. But as her friend, he could warn her about the guy.

Karina made a face. "I don't need your help choosing friends, okay? I don't even know why I came to lunch since you're just going to give me a hard time about what I'm doing. My sister is dead. I have no family left, and you're not the one that's going to fill that gap. Okay? I don't need a brother. Or a babysitter."

Her gaze drifted to the room behind him.. "That girl looks like she's more your speed. And she knows your friends. Go talk to her and leave me alone." She started to shift out of the seat, leaving her soda behind.

The server approached them with a tray of their food.

Liam reached out and touched Karina's arm. "At least take advantage of the fact I'm paying the bill and eat lunch." He gave her arm a gentle squeeze and then let go. If she stayed, it would be because it was her choice. Karina had lost weight since her sister's death, but he'd never seen any signs of drug use on her.

She'd been in the back seat of Morgan's car, not the passenger side. When he'd asked her about it, she'd told him that Morgan had her sit back there because he said she was too distracting to have up front. He didn't buy it. There had been some other inconsistencies—odd things in her story about why she'd been there this morning and other questions she'd backtracked around and flat-out not answered.

Karina sighed and picked up her fork. "Fine, but if you're paying, I'm having extra fries. And dessert."

"Fine by me." He grabbed his burger and took a bite. Then he glanced over to where his brother stood behind the bar and gave him a thumbs-up. He'd added something new to the mayo-based sauce.

Conrad grinned.

Liam spotted Blake and Jasper talking to Blake's sister, Destiny, who stood by their table with her hand on her brother's shoulder but her attention on Jas. Peter Olson, the young guy from Vanguard, stood on the other side of the table in conversation with them, and beside him was...

Her.

When he'd known her in the Marines, she'd been Anne Helton. Now she was Roxie. Another of the lies she was telling everyone.

"Whoa. What was that?"

He turned back to Karina. "What was what?"

"Tough girl over there. What's the deal? Or you don't like that skinny guy?" Karina took a bite of lettuce and chicken while she waited for him to answer.

"The skinny guy is a friend of a friend."

She covered her mouth with her hand, flashing him her manicure. "So it's the girl, then? I said she was your speed. You guys have a thing?"

Minutes ago, she'd been angry-grieving the loss of her sister. Now she was asking about his love life? Or the lack thereof, as the case was.

"There is no *thing*." Never was, never would be. And no need to talk about it either. "I used to know her, that's all."

His mind conjured up images of them in fatigues, sweaty, and laughing their butts off. They'd all run at least six miles that day in full gear—because Liam ordered it and then joined in. But not until everyone had started. Eventually, he'd caught up and overtaken every single one of them. Helton was the one who'd given him a run for his money, flat out sprinting to keep up with him at the end when everyone else hung back.

A smile tugged at his lips, but what was the point? It was just history.

She'd disappeared the minute they'd left the service and finally had the chance to act on the feelings the military hadn't allowed them to indulge. Dropped off the map. He'd tracked her down only to—

Liam cut off his thoughts. "She doesn't mean anything to me."

Karina eyed him like she didn't believe that.

"I mean it. She's nothing."

Better for him to believe that rather than nurse this ridiculous heartache. Until she'd walked back into his life, and he had to face the fact she'd left his heart in pieces. In the weeks since he'd run into her, Liam had doubled down on work. Now the department was taking that away from him as well.

He needed a new direction, or the fact *Roxie* was here would keep tearing him apart.

SIX

Roxie wanted to twist around and wring Peter Olson's neck. Had he known the SWAT guys would be here? They'd talked about having lunch with Liam, for goodness' sake, and now they show up at this spot, and he's here?

Destiny, the server and Blake's sister, smirked at Roxie with a knowing look in her eye.

Blake glanced between them. "What's going on? You guys know each other?"

Roxie frowned. Destiny had just introduced her to Jasper and Blake, Liam's SWAT officers. Peter would have, but she'd beat him to it. "You didn't tell him?"

Destiny's dark-skinned cheeks flushed. "Bro, don't freak out—"

"Every time you say that, my blood pressure rises." Blake was seriously good-looking, even when he despaired over one sister's antics. He had four, so it was a wonder he was even upright at this point. "What is this?"

"I told you I got a roommate."

Roxie glanced at Jasper, who eyed her, then looked at

Liam and whoever he was talking to—having a quiet lunch with. *You don't care, remember?*

Peter chuckled into his glass.

"Blake..." Roxie held out her hand. "I'm Destiny's new roommate."

"*Only* roommate." Destiny grinned. "I don't want another one. You've ruined me. She's a neat freak. She *irons*."

"Old habits."

Blake spun on his stool to Roxie. "Explain."

Before she could, Destiny said, "Some Marine Corps thing, I guess. Liam can probably tell you."

Roxie's stomach clenched.

Jasper said, "You guys knew each other?"

She managed to nod.

"So he'll vouch for you?" Blake asked.

Roxie wasn't going to lie. "No, but he'll tell you the truth."

Blake stared at her.

"So anyway," Destiny began, "I was in the produce section 'cause that's where they put the pico de gallo, and I ran into Rox lookin' at dips. We got to talking. Boom, bing, bang...she's my new roommate."

Blake's ears reddened. She was surprised steam didn't start rising out of them.

"It's been six weeks," Roxie said. "If I haven't murdered her in her sleep by now, she's probably safe."

Destiny said, "She cleans the bathroom. *And* folds my laundry when she needs to put hers in the dryer."

Blake frowned at his sister. "You should do that stuff for yourself."

Destiny waved a hand. Blake geared up for another go at convincing her to be an adult, but she said, "I think I hear another table calling me." She hurried off.

Roxie grinned after her roommate. No joke, they'd hit it

off in about two minutes at the grocery store right after Roxie passed the search and rescue dog handling class she'd taken. She'd come out fully certified but with zero desire to work with a dog when it would only put the dog in danger.

Old wounds, far too exposed to the present.

Jasper watched Destiny leave, which was interesting when added to the way Destiny had glanced at him when her brother wasn't looking. Was there something going on between the SWAT officer and the server?

If so, neither would want Blake to know, but even though secret relationships could be exciting at first, they could turn dangerous pretty quickly.

Roxie shifted her stance and tucked some flyaway strands behind her ear. She didn't care enough to hide her scar. Bangs weren't her thing, they just got in the way. Every time a minute of peace came, all those old emotions snapped back to the surface.

Was she ever going to be able to escape them?

Only if she kept her head down and worked cold cases. Got enough clout with Vanguard that she could pull out the case *she* wanted to work. Clare, the CEO, had interviewed her with Bob Davis—the department head. They'd straight up asked her why she wanted the job when she had no skills for investigation. Her job experience consisted of holding a rifle in the beating sun, watching the backs of the people she worked with, and dog handling—which she didn't want to do now.

Career change, anyone?

She hadn't been offended at the question. Anyone would want to know why she couldn't seem to settle. In a moment of weakness, she'd run down the whole story for them. No point keeping it a secret.

An hour later she was done talking.

Clare had wiped away tears. Bob had cleared his throat. They'd both told her to do the work, learn what she needed to know. And when she had solid footing? They would be right there with her.

Mark wouldn't know what hit him when she showed up with the full force of Vanguard behind her.

"Want some lunch?" Jasper glanced around. "You guys could pull up a table."

Peter started to talk, but she cut him off. "I'm not hungry, and there's work to do."

She stepped back. Being here was far too exposing when Liam sat at a booth with a gorgeous and much younger woman. What did Roxie care? His personal life didn't have anything to do with her, and it never would.

If he'd wanted there to be something between them, then he'd have come and found her. He'd have reached out and asked.

Instead, he'd ghosted her and stayed away.

She took another step back.

Peter held out a hand. "Don't walk into the table behind us."

She glanced at him, no clue what expression she had on her face. Something in the domain of crazy skittish. Fortunately, he'd stopped her from getting hurt and making even more of a scene in front of a bunch of people.

Jasper took a sip of what looked like iced tea. "What case are y'all working?"

As far as she could gather, cops didn't much like private investigators looking into their cases and double-checking their work—finding mistakes. Bob had also explained why a lot of the cops didn't want to contend with him since he represented all the bad eggs in the department. The fact his daughter was an FBI agent in Benson and married to a PD detective did help, though.

The whole community was a sticky web of loyalty and appreciation.

If she had lunch with these guys, got to know them and became friends, she would get stuck in that web. Destiny was the only exception. The one person who saw through all the walls Roxie put up like it was no big deal to connect that deeply after knowing someone such a short time.

As if God wanted her to have a person in her life that she couldn't keep anything from.

Maybe it was true. Destiny seemed to think so. She went to church twice a week, so she should know.

Roxie realized Blake sat there studying her. She glanced at Peter and tuned back into what he was telling Jasper about the homeless guy and the string of deaths. Then Peter said, "We were gonna call Liam since it's connected to his father's death in the line of duty."

Blake straightened. Jasper immediately shook his head. "Don't talk to him about that." He spread both hands and waved, flat palms and fingers straight. "No go."

Right. That made sense. "I was there when his mom called to tell him what happened."

All three guys turned to look at her.

Ack. "So, I can imagine it's still a painful subject."

They'd ended up in a hug on the floor of the common room. He'd been crying, holding on to her so tight she could barely breathe. They'd sat like that awhile until the squad hauled them both up so they could hug him as well. Get him squared away and back to the US so he could take care of his family.

The skin around Jasper's eyes flexed.

"And I should get a to-go order and get back to work." She

made a beeline to the end of the bar, which Destiny wasn't allowed behind because she wasn't twenty-one and couldn't serve alcohol. Her roommate exited the kitchen and met her there.

A handsome man in a Backdraft T-shirt with similar coloring to Liam wandered by. In fact, there were more physical similarities than that.

"Liam's brother, Conrad," Destiny offered. "He and Rory, the other brother, are—what's it called? Irish twins. They were in the same grade, but they're ten months apart in age. Rory runs another Backdraft Bar and Grill in Alaska."

Not that Roxie had asked.

"And that woman Liam is eating with? She's the sister of a confidential informant of his that was killed. He met them both when they were in high school. Arrested their brother for drug dealing, so they went to foster care, and he kept an eye on them. The whole thing is real tragic."

Roxie nodded.

"But you don't need to worry about her. She's not competition." Destiny squeezed her arm.

Roxie frowned. "I'm not worried."

"Because you think nothing is gonna happen?" Destiny grinned. "Why do you think God brought you here?"

Even if He orchestrated this, it didn't have anything to do with romance.

Not anymore.

SEVEN

"They're doing what?" Liam set his hands flat on the table and glanced between Blake and Jasper.

"We didn't want you to hear it from anyone else." Blake held his attention with the steady gaze of a guy who'd watched four younger sisters grow up and done his level best to keep them from harm while they decided what they wanted from their lives. After their father's death and their mother's abandonment, he hadn't let his half-sisters get lost in the system.

A lot like what Liam had tried—and failed—to do with Veronika and Karina.

Jasper said, "We know the file on your father's death. There's nothing to find." He shrugged, not quite using that silver spoon slickness he could employ but close to it.

Jasper was Ivy League and tuxedo.

Liam was blue jeans, boots, and a shotgun.

Blake was a brand-new Camaro, paid for with cash after saving for ten years.

But their team worked. Even with Dakota absent—though by the sound of it he was doing well after rehab, living in Last Chance County. And with their SWAT lieutenant on a desk.

"Where'd they go?" Liam asked.

Blake said, "They got to-go orders from the kitchen and took off."

His brother. "Did they say they were gonna ask Conrad about my dad's death?"

His little brother didn't deserve to be hassled. It didn't matter what Peter and "Roxie," as his teammates called her, had said. It mattered what they'd done before they left.

Stirring up trouble.

She'd gone from leading him on to ignoring him to interfering in his life now. She needed to leave him and his family alone.

Liam strode to the kitchen. He was probably in the clear now that Peter and *Roxie* had left. Karina had finished her salad and nixed the idea of dessert. She'd taken off when her phone buzzed a bunch of times.

He'd told her to put his name down as a reference when she applied for jobs. She'd just waved and strolled out like she had all the time in the world. Veronika hadn't left a life insurance policy. Where was Karina finding the money to get by, to pay her bills?

It would be one of the first questions he asked Morgan Alakov when they got him in an interrogation room the next day. Give the guy a night to sweat and he might think twice about talking in exchange for a deal. Not many in county jail would want a mob-connected Russian in there. Too many other groups wouldn't take kindly to his presence.

He pushed through the swinging door into the kitchen. "Con!"

"By the sauce." His brother's voice came from the right.

Liam headed down the line of silver metal counters, past a

couple of ovens that smelled like the best pizza he'd ever had. Conrad stirred the red sauce pot at the end of the line by the refrigerator.

"Hey."

Conrad glanced over, one brow raised. "What happened?"

The fact he could tell that from one word wasn't something that sat well with Liam. Nor was the fact his eight- and thirteen-year-old nieces smoked him the last time they played dart wars in Conrad's house, like they were trained officers who knew how to rout out a suspect. The eight-year-old would make a decent SWAT officer someday, but he wasn't going to tell Conrad that.

"How's Rory?"

Conrad shrugged. His usual stance over his younger brother. "He's Rory."

The guy ran a franchise of Backdraft Bar and Grill up in Alaska. "Let me know."

Conrad nodded. If Rory needed help, the two of them would head up there and pitch in. Their unwritten rule as brothers.

Liam got down to it. "Did a guy and a woman come in here and talk to you? They're from Vanguard Private Security and Investigation. Digging up stuff that needs to stay buried." For all their sakes, it needed to lie where it was.

Liam could control as much as he was able to, but if someone started shaking trees, things would fall. He wouldn't be able to catch it all.

He ran a hand through his hair, scrubbing at the back of his head. "Anne."

"Who?"

"She's going by Roxie now. She was Anne when I knew her in the Marines." When he'd been so attracted to her he'd hardly been able to see straight. That was then, this was now.

Conrad's eyebrow rose again, and he stopped stirring for a minute. "Okay, what's that about?"

More comfortable than talking about the case being reopened. "She was in my squad." Liam cleared his throat.

"Oh."

"What?"

"You liked her. Still do?" Conrad winced. "Time to fix that mess, bro. What's the problem these days? Both of you are out of the military. Nothing to stop you."

Liam cleared his throat again. What was wrong with him? His brother had found a woman at the end of high school and married her right away, which had been a solid idea since she gave birth five months later and because they were still happy. The girls were great.

Liam had never had a successful relationship in his life. "You wouldn't get it."

"Sure."

Liam frowned.

"Mr. SWAT Team Sergeant. Super cop, kicking in doors and cuffing bad guys."

"And yet I can't seem to get a woman to do more than look twice." Not that this conversation related to Roxie. Their thing was so over it was almost like it had never begun. Liam folded his arms, trying not to be defensive, but this was his brother. Conrad knew.

"It's not about anyone. It's about someone. And I'm guessing it's this Roxie."

"Anne." Why would she have changed her name and then come to his hometown?

"Roxanne?"

Liam frowned. "Huh. Maybe." He'd been so spun out at

seeing her, hearing a new name, he hadn't even put that together. But it was entirely possible. "Okay, so I'm losing my mind."

Conrad grinned. "That means there's something to figure out. If you've barely spoken and you're already losing your mind."

"I don't have time for this." Liam blew out a short breath. "Vanguard is reopening a case related to Dad's death. They're going to pull the file and look over everything."

Between work and family, he hardly had time to worry about Roxie being here. If he was honest, he actually liked that name for her. It suited the woman he'd known, who gave all the guys a run for their money and looked better doing it.

She'd captivated everyone—him especially.

"And you think there's something to find? Maybe there should be." Conrad turned to look at his sauce. "Could be about time."

"It's not good, Con. It's really bad."

"Why?" Conrad looked over. "What's there to find? Dad was shot. The guy who did it died a few days later. What would it hurt to review everything?" He started stirring his sauce again.

"Now it's your turn to spill."

"Because you bared your soul to me over a woman that has you in knots?" Conrad chuckled. He tapped the spoon on the side of the pot and then set it in a dish on the counter by the stove burners. "I'd rather talk about Roxie."

"I'd rather clean up little kid puke."

Conrad grinned, but his expression quickly slipped. "Don't worry, okay? If your police force is as solid as you always say it is, then what is there to be concerned about? Either they won't find anything, or it'll be a truth that needs to come out."

"Why now?" Liam asked. "It's been ten years."

Conrad didn't say anything.

"Talk."

If they'd have been younger, he'd have made a jab about Liam not being his father. Instead, Conrad leaned his hips against the counter. "Mom went to Bob Davis. She wants Vanguard to look at the entire case again. She still doesn't believe it happened exactly as the reports say."

Liam squeezed the bridge of his nose. "Why didn't you tell me?"

"She asked me not to." Conrad squeezed his shoulder. "She knows how you feel."

He'd been at the funeral. As the line of people filed past the coffin, he'd walked out a side door for some air and right into the middle of a conversation between two older cops. A heated conversation.

We both know he was dirty as sin.

He'd shoved at both of them and screamed for them to leave the funeral. Conrad and Rory had dragged him back inside and straightened him out before they went back to face mom.

It was the whole reason he'd joined the Benson Police Department. So he could walk in his father's footsteps...

No matter where that led him.

EIGHT

Roxie held a tight leash on her frustration. "So you have zero records at all?"

The receptionist, who was not at fault and just trying to do her job at Hurstwhile Treatment Center, shook her head. All that perfectly curled blonde hair didn't even move. "There was a cyberattack on the company. Some kind of ransomware a few years ago. It wiped out all our records, so I'm afraid everything from before wasn't recovered. We had to start over and rebuild the system—and all the patient records."

And the homeless guy had been seen here prior to that. "What about any staff that worked here and saw or treated him?"

"I'm sure you're not asking me to break patient confidentiality."

HIPAA rules applied until fifty years after a person's death. Which was far too long to wait for answers. Maybe the next of kin—the niece, Turner—would allow them to access medical information. "No, I'm not. I'm simply trying to get an overview of how a place like this works."

Hurstwhile had contracts with the VA to treat retired

servicemen and servicewomen. They were pretty well known in the northwest, and being located just outside Benson but close to the freeway gave people easy access to the center.

Roxie watched the receptionist's expression shutter. "I'll let you get back to work. Here's my card. If you or anyone you work with is available to provide my company with context for our investigation, we'd appreciate it." She left the card on the counter, figuring it would get thrown away as soon as the automatic doors slid closed.

She stepped out into the late afternoon light. Nearly time to quit, but she'd so rarely worked jobs that had a nine-to-five aspect to them that she barely considered what a normal workday looked like.

Her car was across the lot because that was the only empty space she could find. Peter had opted to do more work online. It was a huge part of his skill set, and he'd wanted to get into the ME reports about the deaths that his brother thought were connected somehow.

Skin on the back of her neck prickled.

Roxie reached for the gun on her hip but didn't slide it out. In someone's crosshairs wasn't a good place to be now, or anytime. In the Marines, she'd occasionally been a target someone tried to take out, but right now, she didn't even have the guys she'd rolled out with to back her up.

After leaving the Marines, she'd ended up in a life she never wanted and shouldn't have fallen into.

Now that life—that man—had her in his sights again.

She walked calmly to her car. When would he make his move? She checked the back seat and lay on the asphalt to look under the car. No assailant or device that might explode when she turned on the ignition. When nothing else happened, she started the car and pulled out. Every second of the drive, she checked her rearview, then the side mirrors.

Constant vigilance grew exhausting fast, so she headed home rather than back to the office. She could text Bob and tell him she'd knocked off when she got there.

The knot in her stomach tightened. She should eat something since she'd barely touched her lunch after all that happened at Backdraft, but there was no way she'd be able to keep it down.

Roxie ran her fingers down the scar on the side of her face. He'd left her for dead once, why couldn't he do it again? Was that really too much to ask? But of course, it was. Mark had a sick obsession with her, and she would always be caught in his mess—unless she managed to burn the whole thing down and him with it. Maybe her, too, but at least it would be over.

She pulled into the driveway of Destiny's townhouse. A red truck was parked at the curb. As she climbed out of her little SUV, Liam got out of the truck.

She looked back in her car at the empty seat she'd been sitting in and let out a breath. She whispered, "I can't do this right now."

She ended up leaning in for her backpack on the passenger seat instead of going around. That would have put her on the same side as him, rather than with her car between them.

When she straightened, slinging her backpack on her shoulders like all this was no big deal, he was at the back corner. Was she supposed to say, "Hey?"

"*Roxie.*"

Ack. That tone. "Hello, Liam." No longer constrained by his rank or last name, she could experience the feel of his name on her tongue.

She glanced around at the street, making sure whoever had been watching her at Hurstwhile wasn't hanging around still, planning to pick her off. They could hit Liam instead, and Benson PD would erupt if one of their sergeants was hurt or killed.

Roxie headed for the hood of her car. "Let's go inside."

She didn't really need to invite him in, but he clearly had something to say, and he'd been waiting for her. She respected who he was far too much not to give him that. The fact her heart would be breaking the entire time was something she'd just have to deal with.

She used her key, then called out, "Destiny!" in case her roommate had come home already.

No answer. Was that good or bad?

She dumped her backpack in the hallway instead of taking it to her room. "Would you like a drink? Some coffee?" She headed for the kitchen since it wasn't far.

"This won't take that long."

She winced because he couldn't see her face, then blanked her expression and turned, leaning the side of her hip against the end of the counter for support. "What can I help you with?"

His expression flexed, just a tiny shift of the skin around his eyes. "I know what case you're working on. I know why."

She said nothing.

"Leave it alone. The past doesn't need to get dragged up at this point. It's over. Who cares what happened to a homeless guy who *shot my father in the back*? The man just OD'd. Probably out of an abundance of guilt."

She stared at him, remembering that hug on the floor the moment after he found out about his father's death. That guy who had clung to her was so different from this man. Years had passed, and it was like he had turned to stone. There was a hardness to him now that hadn't been there before.

She tried to keep her voice steady. "I can pass that on to

Bob, but I don't really get a say in what I work. I'm too new with the company."

"Why did you come here?" Liam stared at her in a way that made her want to crack. It probably worked great on criminals. "You knew that I live here."

And it had seemed like a good place to start over, but not just because of that tiny flicker of hope inside her that she could have the impossible thing she wanted. "The Search and Rescue training center."

"And now Vanguard. Didn't you pass Mitchell's course?"

"I got certified."

"And you're working for Vanguard now, not as a dog handler?"

She swallowed. "It's..." No words came for an explanation, and why did he need to know anyway? It was her business, and they weren't part of each other's lives. It wasn't like he actually cared about her. "It's my choice. My life. I'm not living beholden to someone else's whims." Not anymore.

"The Marine Corps wasn't that bad, was it?"

It hadn't been bad at all. Her life as a marine had given her a clarity of purpose. These days, she was adrift, getting tossed around with no clue how to navigate anything.

All she could do was shake her head while the sheen of tears burned her eyes.

"Roxie?" He took a small step toward her.

The doorbell rang.

She flinched so hard he reached out a hand toward her.

"I'll get it." Liam strode to the door. She rushed after him in time to see him fling the door open so hard it hit the stopper. "It's just a package." He bent to pick it up.

"Don't!" She ran over and grabbed his belt, tugging him back.

Liam stumbled, caught himself, and straightened. "What? What is this?"

Her breath came hard now, each inhale and exhale. Sharp and fast so her head spun.

He set his hands on her shoulders. "Roxie, hold your breath for a second. Slow it down." All she could do was exactly what he asked. "Good, now tell me what this is."

A tear slid from the corner of her eye. "Don't open it."

NINE

Liam realized he was touching her and dropped his hands. This woman could always get behind whatever walls he put up, whatever guard he tried to use to protect the soft parts inside him that she'd bruised and torn apart when she walked away. When she'd tossed him aside. "What makes you think that is anything other than a regular delivery?"

Could be something from that megastore online for all they knew. Completely harmless. And yet, she acted like it could be a bomb about to explode.

"Do I need to call the bomb squad?"

She winced. "I don't know."

The scar on the side of her face wasn't from her time as a marine. "Has it happened before?"

She inhaled a long, shuddering breath.

"That's it." He pulled his phone out. "I'm making the call." They didn't have a designated bomb squad full-time—part of the reason the commissioner was disbanding SWAT for a collateral duty team that worked on call was so they could be cross-trained. But there were officers and firefighters who formed a group with the skill and the equipment to do this.

"No!" She pretty much yelled in his face, more fear than he'd ever seen in her, and they'd been in some scary situations. "Don't." She sucked in a breath. "I'll check it."

"I will. Or both of us." There were things they could do. He had a few things in his truck, but equipment that would sense an explosive device wasn't something he kept on hand—nor was a bomb-sniffing dog.

She headed for the door. "It's unlikely that it's an explosive."

And yet, she'd protected him like he might die and apparently she couldn't stand that. An entirely confusing thought, considering he otherwise believed she didn't care one whit about him. But then, he'd never understood women, and that wasn't likely to suddenly occur now.

"Even so..."

"We don't have hours to wait."

"Unless you have a bomb dog in your room, we'll have to deal with it."

She glanced back over her shoulder, all that bravado gone. "I would never put a dog in danger like that. It could get hurt —or die!"

So he was as valuable to her as an animal? Oddly, that took some of the pressure off figuring out her minor freak-out. "Back up. Let me see it."

Was it worth the risk? Maybe not. But she was right that they didn't need to spend hours wasting people's time if there was no reason to believe this was an explosive. He pulled his pen flashlight out. The four sides of the box were overlapped, folded into each other. This wasn't a package delivery.

He clicked the flashlight on and aimed it at the open slit.

The box shifted.

"Whoa." Liam caught himself before he toppled back. "Let's take a look."

He hooked the flashlight in the open slot and flipped it up. A snake hissed, then lifted its head so that it rose slowly toward the opening. Uncurling. Beady eyes, taking in its surroundings.

Liam slammed the flaps down, knocking it back in. He held it closed with the flashlight and blew out a long breath. "Animal control." He still had his phone handy and made the call. When he'd hung up, he said, "Roxie, get me something to set on the lid so it can't get out." She didn't reply. He glanced over his shoulder. "Roxie?"

She appeared, face pale and eyes wide. Totally in shock. She handed over a book—a Bible. "Like this?" Her voice shook.

"Thanks." His Bible sat dusty on his shelf at home. This one looked like it had been appreciated and enjoyed for years. Was it hers? He set the book on the box and straightened, turning to the door just as it slammed in his face.

He lifted his fist and knocked. "Roxie!"

No answer.

He hammered. Rang the bell. "Roxie!" He needed to know she hadn't passed out. "I'm calling an ambulance, and I will break this door down if you don't answer me."

"It isn't locked." Her voice sounded muffled.

Liam twisted the handle and entered. He found her on the floor in the hall, back to the wall and her knees up. The strong soldier he knew looked so small sitting there that he wanted to scoop her up and hold on to her.

Instead, he crouched to do a visual assessment of her shock symptoms. He would've called an ambulance if he didn't know she'd been a marine. Instead, he asked, "A snake?"

Her entire body shuddered.

"Okay, okay." He winced. "We won't talk about the box."

"You should go." She gasped, trying to rally herself. "I'll deal with animal control."

She really thought he'd voluntarily leave her like this? "I'll deal with them. I called it in." Sounded official, and she might be out of it enough not to argue. "I'm not going anywhere."

He figured embarrassment would win out over the shock, and after he'd come here to get her to agree to leave his father's case alone, he hadn't expected to land in the middle of something else entirely.

Something that might explain a few things.

He watched her settle. The faraway look in her eyes started dissipating in place of the focus he was more familiar with. Then again, he'd seen intensity in her eyes, which was his favorite.

No, he didn't need to remember what drew him to her.

She was in the middle of something, and he had plenty to occupy him. Maybe the timing never would've been right for them. It was probably pointless to try now, even if it was possible to get past everything. Why go for it when the end result would inevitably be failure? He didn't like losing.

"Tell me what's going on?" Liam spoke softly, using the tone he applied to situations with traumatized victims. "Who sent that box?"

She only shook her head in a jerky move. Then she looked at the open door and the box.

"It's not coming out." Liam paused. "I do need you to tell me what this is." Someone was targeting her. He could guess, but he needed the truth and not conclusions that would color how he went forward. He'd be working on assumptions, not facts. "Roxie?"

She lifted her gaze to his. "That is my name."

He frowned.

"Roxanne."

"But you were Anne."

"And now I'm Roxie." She sniffed. "I like it better."

"It does suit you." But why had she opted for another name in the Marine Corps? Rather than ask, he said, "I'd like to help you. If you'll let me."

He was a cop. But that didn't automatically mean people trusted him. Used to be it was more of a given that cops could be trusted. Lately, less so. Though, only because of the few bad eggs. He didn't worry about it elsewhere, just Benson. And even here there had been dirty cops—Hank Maxwell had been a killer.

No one wanted a repeat of that.

Or the rest of it, which was far too close to home.

Roxie shook her head slightly. "You can't help me."

"We can get you a restraining order. There are things you can do, and I know you know how to protect yourself." She worked for Vanguard. Surely they'd assign operatives to protect her if they knew of the situation, wouldn't they? He'd rather do it himself, but his work schedule was killer on a good week. Lately, with trying to take down a dangerous Russian family, things were even worse. He came home late every night to an empty house. A dog might help, but that would only end in animal neglect.

"That won't work," she said.

"I know it's just a piece of paper, but it protects your right to be safe." Liam touched her fingers with his, wanting to hold her hand. But if he did that, he might never let go. "I can help you."

"No one can." She sniffed. "You don't think I've tried."

He studied the scar on her forehead. "He hurt you."

A tear rolled down her cheek. She swiped it away before he could.

"I'm not going to walk away knowing it might happen again. Who is he? Tell me, and I'll make it so you don't have to be scared anymore." A protective swell rose in him, far more powerful than anything he'd felt before. He needed to safeguard her.

"You can't."

He started to speak, but she cut him off.

"No one can. Because he's dead."

TEN

Roxie was drinking coffee the next morning at the breakfast bar when Destiny got up. Didn't matter how late the girl worked, she always got up before seven.

In time to see the suitcase and the duffel packed and waiting in the hall by the front door.

Destiny strode down the hall and stopped at the door to the kitchen. "Vacation?" The one word contained so much sarcasm it was obvious Destiny offered that option because it was the farthest from the truth.

"I'll pour you some coffee. We can talk about—"

"Woman, you sit back down." Destiny headed for the coffee pot herself. "Because you aren't going anywhere, so you can unpack those bags before you go to work. Or better yet, take the day off, stay here, and watch movies. We can plan a bestie vacation of our own."

Roxie stalled her mug before she could take a sip. "I don't think I even know how to take a vacation." She'd had leave before, but had she ever actually taken a day off on purpose?

"And I don't think I've been at Vanguard long enough for that."

Destiny drank some coffee. She had on shorts and a tank top, displaying all that gorgeous dark skin with no scars whatsoever. Because why would she have any? This woman was smarter than Roxie. Just as strong, but life hadn't led her to make the poor decisions Roxie had—more than once, in fact.

Not that Destiny had ever had it easy. She'd been working as a server since she turned fourteen and was currently going to school and working. Paying her way with the money she made —which Roxie was happy to ease by contributing to the rent.

"I'm not going to put you in danger." Roxie wasn't budging about this. "I won't let him hurt you."

"So, you being miserable and alone is the answer?"

"I'll be safe and so will you." Roxie set her mug down. This home hadn't been hers for long, but it was the nicest one she'd ever been in. Only a couple of years since it had been built. Furnished with comfort in mind and a little of Destiny's bold colors, soft blankets style. "You need a cat."

"A dog would have fought the snake if it attacked you."

Roxie slid off the stool. "I'm going to work." And she was taking her stuff with her, which meant she wouldn't be back. "I just want to say thank you for everything you've—"

"Save it. Because we're not breaking up."

"I've never had a best friend." Liam was probably the closest thing she'd ever had to one. "You set the bar high." Roxie walked down the hall, grabbed her things, and loaded them into the back of her car.

Peter was parked at the curb beside the end of the driveway.

He waved, then gave her a hand signal.

Roxie lifted her chin. Good thing he wasn't closer, or he'd

see how choked up she was right now. All because Vanguard —or just Peter—had decided she needed a protection detail on the drive to the office. She wasn't alone and didn't need to be. She had a support system.

Except it didn't include Liam O'Connell and those brooding blue eyes or the mega tree trunks he called arms. That expansive chest.

She rolled her eyes and focused on the drive instead of the distracting specimen of police officer. It wasn't polite to ogle, even in her memories. Roxie tried not to be a cliché, but when a guy looked like that...and worse, didn't even realize it, what was she supposed to do? Everything in her took notice.

The only problem? Every single time in her life that had happened, what came after it was nothing but pain.

Reason wanted her to believe Liam might be nothing like the others. He might be a good guy. A safe guy. He'd never done anything to make her believe he wasn't trustworthy.

But her heart couldn't afford to take the risk.

She parked close by the building and shut the car off. Peter stood scanning around them, close by the door when she got out. He walked beside her to the front door.

She said nothing as they tapped their badges to the entry scanner and nothing as they stepped into the elevator. When the doors slid closed, she turned to him. "Destiny should go stay with her brother, or we should get someone to sit on the house, right?"

"I looped in Blake. He's up to speed—" She was about to interrupt to ask about Liam when he quickly added, "With the agreement that he not share outside of his sister. And she already knows."

Roxie nodded. Destiny knew it all— even more than what she'd told Clare and Bob at her interview.

"We offered a detail. Blake is going to cover it himself, and he'll let us know if he needs anything."

The doors slid open.

Bob stuck his head out of his office, lifted his chin, and then disappeared.

"We should put cameras in at Destiny's house."

"That's a good idea. You can do it when you take your stuff back there later."

She flinched, then just kept going so she turned all the way around to face him. "He knows where I live."

"You knew it was a risk." Peter held her attention with the steady gaze of a guy who'd seen more than most. "So why did you move in?"

"Because I was stupid."

He shook his head. "It's because you had hope."

"That's gone now. It's over." She dumped her backpack at her desk and slumped into her chair, then leaned forward with her forearms on her knees. "I can't go back there."

Blake would tell Liam, no matter what he'd promised. If Liam hadn't looked her up already and found reports that amounted to the apparent ramblings of a crazy person, he'd hear it from his SWAT teammate.

They would realize how impossible it was going to be to keep everyone safe. The best course of action would be for her to bunk down here, maybe in the break room. Shower here. Eat here. Work here. Wait it out. Let Mark get so frustrated with her being out of reach that he made a misstep. Slipped up and exposed himself.

"Let's get to work." Peter settled into his own chair. "We have a meeting in ten, and we can figure this out by end of day, right?"

He played it off, but she got the idea he had something cooking.

At the end of the day, she was probably going to wind up in a safe house or somewhere else not of her choosing. That wasn't going to work for her. She wouldn't be a captive in her own life.

Not again.

"Hi, Ms. Turner. Can you hear me?"

Roxie slid her chair over to sit beside Peter so she could talk to Sierra as well. Though she hadn't had time to mull it over—what with the snake and having to explain why she wasn't going to file a police report—she was still looking into a case related to Liam's father's death. How they handled it mattered.

The woman on-screen wore a pink scrubs top with flowers on it. "I can see and hear you."

Roxie said, "We appreciate your time."

Sierra Turner, the niece of the homeless OD victim, lifted a mug with a tea tag wrapped around the handle. Behind her was what looked like a hotel room or a hospital waiting area. Maybe a quiet place to chat since she was on shift. "I gave up a while ago wondering when someone would ask questions about what happened. Seems like no one cared that I didn't agree."

Roxie said, "After he died, did you ever look at copies of his medical information?"

There were more questions than that to ask, but considering her career field, it was a good place to start.

Sierra nodded. "I had the ME walk me through the report he made, and I tried to get him to do an autopsy. He didn't see a reason to, and I didn't have the money to pay for it."

Peter leaned forward in his chair. "But you got the impression there was more to the story than what the police reports said?"

"My uncle shouldn't have been on the streets. He was

supposed to be in a treatment program, and the idea he would kill that cop? It's unbelievable." She shook her head. "He called me a few days before. He sounded...better. Like things were working."

"I'm sorry for your loss." Roxie had to say it.

"No one has ever said that to me. Not once." Sierra rubbed her nose. "So, thank you."

Peter said, "Have you looked into the center where he was supposed to be in treatment?"

"I went by and tried to talk to them. I applied for a job there when they had an opening for an RN a couple of years ago. They never called me in for an interview even." Sierra sighed. "I've looked into them, but they're pretty closed mouthed. The one time I was supposed to go to coffee with a nurse who worked there, she never showed. I don't know what else I could've done."

Roxie said, "We're going to look into it."

"Thank you." Sierra's expression washed with relief. "Thank you."

ELEVEN

Morgan Alakov shuffled in his orange jumpsuit and white canvas shoes to the end of the cafeteria line and headed for the tables. More than one group watched him go, evil intention in their eyes. He'd been fighting since he was old enough to stand upright on his own, scrapping with everyone who wanted to fight him and bleeding for every ounce of respect he'd earned.

For example, the way the table of Russians watched with an entirely different expression. He lifted his chin as he headed toward them, then at the last second, set his tray down in front of an older man with thinning hair and big glasses.

"Don't sit here." His voice shook.

Morgan planted his behind on the bench but didn't start eating. The man across from him had been trading with other inmates for extra pudding by the look of it. That might give him something to bargain with if it came down to it. "Time to talk."

"I'm eating."

"I'm not here for the mashed potatoes." Sure, he'd had a warrant out for his arrest, but there was a reason the cops had found him this morning. The fact Karina had been in the car might've put a wrench in things, depending on how smart that cop was, the one who thought he was her big brother. And depending on how well she could keep her mouth shut.

The man across from him was the best chemist in the Pacific Northwest, and nothing he did was legit.

"You know who I work for." Morgan pushed up his sleeve so the chemist could see the bratva tattoo he'd worn so long it was faded. "So you can probably guess why I'm here."

Someone walked by, close enough they were clearly trying to hear what he and the chemist were saying. Did this man across from him have an agreement with someone else in this room—another group he was going to work for?

Morgan would kill whoever that was, but drawing attention like that was bad for business. No one needed the media in an uproar about a death in county lockup. Not after his family had murdered another man in a police station in Benson a few months ago—a betrayal Raphi was *not* happy about.

The killer had been killed by the cops, case closed. Except Raphi's own brother had been the one who'd done it...before his death. No one had expected Nico's play for the crown. Or what he'd done to get their father's watch from his corpse.

Raphi had been livid. He'd murdered one of his favorite girlfriends in a fit of rage, strangling her to death. Morgan had disposed of the body as ordered, because it was never worth crossing Raphi when he was like that.

Now the man was in charge of the family. There was no telling him no. Ever.

Things would be like this from now on, and it was up to them all to get used to it.

The chemist swallowed a bite of beef and gravy that he'd swiped through mash. Morgan's stomach flipped over. The chemist shrugged. "You want me to come up with something for you. Something special?"

He wasn't here for whatever the chemist might have cooking in his brain. They didn't deal with long shots like that. "Nope."

The chemist's brows flickered. "Then what?" He was definitely intrigued, which was good for business. He'd be motivated to do the work out of curiosity, plus the payout Raphi was working on.

"I want you to finish something that was started." Morgan reached into his pocket and pulled out a folded piece of paper. He slid it across the table. "Solve a puzzle for us. We'll make it worth your while."

The chemist stared. Didn't want to seem too eager. Then he snatched the paper and unfolded it. Took a few minutes of muttering, rotating the paper for some reason, a grunt. He frowned, then stared at it with his mouth open. "Interesting."

Across the room, someone got up and headed for them. One of the Hispanics. A couple of his guys intercepted the man and began a heated conversation. He needed to get this done before something kicked off in here and dinner got cut short.

"Can you solve it?"

The chemist looked from the paper to him. "What if I turn down this offer?"

As far as the Russians were concerned, there was no turning them down. "We take what you hold most dear."

"I have no family."

Morgan shook his head. "Not a person. A storage unit in Olympia. Mint condition, cherry red, 1966 Shelby Mustang. It's a GT350-H four-speed isn't it?"

The chemist swallowed.

"I've never burned a vintage car before. Should be fun."

His lips thinned. No point saying, "You wouldn't," since they very much would.

Morgan said, "I want an answer."

Extra guards came into the room. His men sat back down, but only after Morgan gave them a nod. The chemist was coming around.

"What happened to whoever came up with this?" The chemist folded the paper back up and tucked it in a pocket. "Why can't he help you?"

"Don't worry about him. Worry about you, and your car." Morgan didn't need the guy to do anything, just solve that equation and give them something new to work with. A breakthrough to advance work that had been going on for years.

If they could crack this code, there would be no stopping Raphi's plan. The old man was dead in that limo bombing. Raphi's brother Nico was dead. No one lived that could challenge him.

"How much will I be paid?"

Morgan picked up his fork. "How much do you want?"

"And what did you hear them say?" Liam stood across a table in a county jail interview room where convicts usually met with their lawyers. In this case, he needed his old "friend" to spill about the guy Morgan had been talking to.

They'd seen the whole conversation from the hub in the office where they watched it play out on the surveillance cameras that covered nearly every inch of this place.

What they didn't know was the words exchanged between the two.

His old "friend" Skippy sniffed. "Nothin'. He just handed the guy a paper."

Jasper pushed off the wall. "Did you see what was on it?"

Skippy looked at him, then at Liam. "Who's the pretty boy?"

"Just answer the question, Skip," Liam said.

"Did you tell him I beat you out for football captain junior year? You tell him that? How I ran more yards and scored more touchdowns. How the coach said I was the one who was gonna go pro." He slapped a hand on his chest even though they were cuffed to the waist belt that shackled him to himself —hands and feet.

"No, I didn't tell Officer Hollingsworth that neither of us went pro, Skip." Liam shifted his stance, the weight of his uniform belt creaking. "What was on the paper?"

"Bunch of numbers."

"Like algebra?" Jasper frowned. "An equation?"

"How am I supposed to know?" Skippy turned to Liam like *Where did you get this guy?*

Liam asked, "Who is he?"

"I don't know." Skippy sniffed again. "Been keepin' my nose clean so that I can get out. Gonna take my girl to Tampa."

"Good." Liam nodded. "You should do that."

"Can I go now?"

"Did you hear anything else?"

Skippy shrugged as much as he could with the shackles. "He told the old guy to solve it."

Liam glanced at Jasper. They needed the information one of the officers was currently digging up on the man Morgan had spoken to. Namely, who he was and why he'd been sentenced here.

Meanwhile, all Liam could think about was the look on Roxanne's face the night before. She was both women—the one he'd known years ago and the person she was now. Two facets of her personality. He'd seen both. Before and after the snake delivery.

What he didn't understand was why she'd refused to make a police report. Didn't she know that was how they established a pattern of this man's actions in order to bring charges? Every threat toward her meant a nail in his coffin— figuratively, anyway. Did she not want to bring the guy down?

Without her telling him the guy's name, he had no way to figure out who it was.

Because he's dead.

"Later, Lee." Skippy headed out of the room with a guard, who gave Liam a confused look.

Liam didn't blame the guy. Skippy acted like they were friends when Liam was the one who'd arrested him for social security fraud—cashing his dead grandma's checks.

Jasper said, "You wanna pull Morgan in here?"

Liam scratched the stubble on his jaw. "Yeah, but I want info on the other guy first." He headed out to the hall and back to the main hub of offices. The surveillance rooms were in the center with the inmates separated into smaller pods surrounding them. They located the officer currently tasked with pulling up information on the convict Morgan had spoken with.

"Ah, there you are." The officer turned in his chair. "I was just about to come find you guys."

Jasper said, "Here we are," and headed for the coffeemaker.

"Oscar Prentiss is currently incarcerated in this fine establishment because of failure to report everything on his state taxes, failure to pay alimony, and the attempted kidnapping of a Chihuahua."

Liam blinked.

Jasper nearly choked on his coffee. "How does that help?"

The officer pointed at Jasper. "Exactly. That's what I thought. So, I did some digging into his files. The divorce occurred because Oscar was apparently testing drugs he was making in his kitchen on the dog."

Liam frowned.

"Nothing came of it. The evidence was destroyed before the techs got in there. He cleaned it up good. All they had was the statement of a disgruntled spouse and a dog that suffered no ill effects. In fact, Oscar said the dog liked getting high."

"I find that hard to believe."

The officer grinned. "I know, right?" He sighed out a long breath. "Seems like he's got some skill with substances."

"What about his career?"

"He worked for a startup company developing a supplement drink. It was turned into a multilevel marketing scheme, but the whole thing went belly up a couple of years ago." The officer shrugged. "Didn't work. Made a few people sick. A lady sued them because she gained ten pounds."

Jasper said, "Huh."

Liam made notes on his phone. "So, the Russians need something from a guy with the scientific know-how to create drug cocktails from scratch in his kitchen."

"At least the subject lived." Jasper grinned over his mug, but it wasn't funny. No one wanted another spate of drug overdoses.

There was entirely enough of that already. As far as dealers were concerned, death was bad for business.

What did Morgan want Oscar to do?

Solve it.

"Pull Morgan," he told the officer. "I wanna talk to him."

The officer stood. "I'll let my sergeant know."

A few minutes later, they were in the same room where they'd spoken to Skippy when an officer led a shackled Morgan Alakov into the room. He caught sight of them and made a face. "You guys."

"Sorry you're so disappointed."

Morgan slumped into the chair and used his hands between his knees to scoot up to the table. "Today hasn't been all bad."

So Oscar had agreed. "You'll be here for a long time. No

bail, you're a flight risk. You won't see the outside of a cell for a long time to come."

"So? I've made peace with my fate." Morgan stared down his nose at them, which was pretty impressive from a seated position.

"Just like that, you're gonna give up everything? Take the hit and sit here for decades to come. No fight?" Liam stared right back.

Jasper sipped his coffee as if they had all day.

"What's my other option?" He looked like a man expecting to be handed a favor.

"You want a sweet deal, then you talk to the prosecutor. But I can't convince her to lessen the charges or shorten her recommended sentence unless you give me something that will carry weight with her."

Liam folded his arms and shrugged. Nothing to offer the guy.

Unless he coughed up.

Would it be about the paper he'd handed Oscar—or something else?

"What do you want to know?"

Liam hated the dance as much as he loved it. "Where do I find Raphi Obolensky?"

"Look him up in the phone book."

"I know where he lives. Where do I find him?"

Morgan grinned. "Might as well ask about the Tooth Fairy. You aren't gonna find him." He leaned forward. "Because you don't find Raphi. Raphi finds you." He sat back and tipped his head back, cracking up with laughter at his own joke.

"Then get a message to him that I wanna talk." Liam shrugged one shoulder again, like it was nothing to him.

"What does he want to talk with a cop for?"

"Just tell him it's me asking."

"So he knows you're coming, and he can be ready with a hit squad?" Morgan grinned. "'Cause that's the only meeting you're gonna have with an Obolensky."

"I think he'll talk to me."

Morgan's eyes narrowed. Liam knew something he didn't, and this guy wanted to know what it was because it irked him that he didn't. "What do you have going with Raphi?"

"That's between him and me."

Morgan obviously didn't want to get lost in the shuffle, written off as inconsequential. But his face stayed an impassive mask. "So go see him. What do I care? I'm sure he'll have something special planned for you."

"What does Raphi want with Oscar?"

Morgan shrugged. "How should I know?"

Maybe he didn't know and was quickly realizing he was the middleman. Liam said, "Where is he?"

"Café Pietro." Morgan lifted his chin. "Tell him I said to kill you slow."

Fifteen minutes later, they were on their way out the doors, and Liam was returning a missed call.

"Something up?"

He shook his head in response to Jasper's question. "Buddy of mine in Marine Intelligence."

The call connected. "O'Connell, how the heck are you?"

Liam grinned. "Good. You got my message?"

"Sure did." He whistled. "Buddy, you need to stay away from Roxanne Helton. She's bad news, man. *Unstable.* If you get my meaning. Steer clear of that mess."

"Anything on the guy she said came after her?"

"The *dead* guy?" His buddy laughed. "Killed while on

leave in South Carolina. Car accident. The body was burned beyond recognition. Shoot, if it is suspicious, she's probably the one who did it."

THIRTEEN

"Thanks." Roxie hung up the desk phone and turned in her chair.

"You got something?" Peter leaned back in his, close enough to reach out to each other but not so close they'd bump each other's chairs. "That sounded promising."

She nodded because the conversation with a civilian employee at the police department had given her information they needed. "The nurse who was supposed to meet Sierra Turner, the one who worked at Hurstwhile, was in their database. The night before they were meant to have coffee, she got in a traffic accident. She died. That's why she was a no-show."

Peter's eyebrows rose.

Like always, there was something in his expression she didn't normally see in civilians. She usually saw it in people she'd served with, who had seen the kind of crazy stuff she had. Horror, terror. All those things. When it hammered at your psyche in the relentless way war did, it sank into your soul. There was no stopping it.

Peter had seen things. He'd experienced real fear and pain.

It might seem strange to a lot of people, but it was easier to trust someone like him. They'd clicked in a way that made him a friend and not just a colleague. He had a girlfriend, so he was safe in a lot of ways. Easy to be around.

Roxie got her thoughts back on track. "The death was ruled an accident. The car exploded when it went over the edge where there's no barrier and landed in the river, burning the body beyond recognition. The report said it was like nothing the responding state police officer had ever seen."

"Whoa."

She nodded. "The police never dug deeper than what it appeared to be, which was a tragic accident. And I can't really blame them. There was nothing about it that indicated foul play or gave them suspicion of it."

Peter shrugged one shoulder. "Same with William Lincoln Turner. No one looked below the surface."

"If we're going to start claiming there's more to it, then we're the ones who will have to dig. We'll have to find something concrete that connects them. Something to convince the police to reopen these old cases as homicides."

And what was the likelihood they'd be inclined to do that with deaths that occurred years ago. There were plenty of open cases now. People in imminent danger. Killers roaming the streets because the police were still compiling evidence.

If they brought up these old cases, it could mean the police shifted resources to work those, and a dangerous person could be on the streets even minutes longer than they would've been otherwise. Roxie, of all people, knew how much could happen in a matter of minutes.

She'd been left for dead.

"You okay?"

She managed to nod...and resist the need to run a finger

down her temple over the scar Mark had given her. "Yep. What do we do now?"

"I'm looking into Hurstwhile. Since it's a nonprofit, a lot of their information is public record." He turned and scooted toward his computer. "It's all in the file, but basically, their financials look a little too clean. Simon is working on breaking into their system. We'll see how that goes. The owner is a corporation that's owned by another corporation. There's a figurehead, but we're not sure how to get ahold of him. Might even be a fake identity, or some kind of pseudonym."

She pulled it up on hers and spotted a familiar name immediately. "They wanted to partner with the Ridgeman Center in Last Chance County?"

"Sounds like it." Peter wheeled his chair over to beside her. "They wanted to combine their efforts in working with veterans. Provide more comprehensive care because they could share best practices and what they've learned."

"Sounds like a great way to level up."

"Right."

"And it didn't go through?" Roxie glanced over.

Peter gave her a sharp shake of his head. "Nope. Clare gave me Dean Cartwright's number since they know each other—that's the guy who ran the Ridgeman Center—and he said he didn't get a good feeling. He didn't dig. He just didn't have a peace about it, so he declined the offer."

"Huh." Roxie knew Dean personally. She could've made that call. But Peter hadn't known enough about her history to make the offer. He'd used the resources he had available. "Good for Dean, if it turns out something more is going on."

"Something more is *always* going on."

Roxie grinned. "Sure seems like it."

"You know the Ridgeman Center?"

Such an innocent question, and everything in her tensed. "I do." She took a breath. "I've stayed there."

Peter nodded, a knowing look on his face. "They're good people."

"Yes, they are."

"One of Liam's guys on SWAT went there a few months ago. Dakota. He stayed in Last Chance County afterward, and he told me they really helped him. He's clean now and part of a Bible study."

She nodded. "They like to push the faith angle with their program."

One of his brows rose. "You didn't like that part?"

Roxie cringed. "It isn't that. I'd never really thought about faith as something that would help me. Seems more like a bunch of rules and being told what you *shouldn't* do. And then the people who are supposed to follow all that do whatever they want, until they're caught, and then they're all sorry about it." She shrugged. "I just never resolved all that."

"Faith isn't about other people," Peter said gently. "It's about you and God, and there's no one else in that mix. You have to decide for yourself what you're going to do about Him."

For the most part, she'd ignored the issue. Lived her life.

One day, probably soon, she was going to have to face what she'd pushed away in favor of denial. Destiny had tried to get her to do so. Liam had as well, even. Back when they'd been friends.

Roxie sighed.

"Helton!"

She glanced over at Bob, who'd stuck his head out of his office. "Yeah, boss?"

He grinned. "Clare wants to see you upstairs!" He disappeared back into his office, but not before she saw a flush on his face. He liked being the boss? She didn't blame him for basking in her respect after what he'd been through and how far he'd strayed.

As far as she was concerned, he'd earned it.

Roxie opted for the stairs and spotted Simon on the landing by the door to the main floor. "Everything okay?"

He nodded, his long hair moving over his shoulders. "Just taking a break."

She squeezed his elbow. "Go see Peter."

Roxie could read him a little better than she normally could with acquaintances since she'd spent time around his twin brother, but it still wasn't clear what was going on with him. When she opened the door, she turned and saw him heading downstairs.

She made her way to Clare's office, which was guarded by Lena at the desk out front. Roxie offered her a smile. "Clare asked me up."

Lena's return smile was completely fake. "You can go right in."

Roxie knocked, regardless. She waited until Clare called out, "Enter," and then she stepped into the office. Bigger than any commander's office she'd ever been in. This one had a bathroom, and rumor had it there was a back stairwell to an apartment upstairs.

Clare got up from behind her desk, her wedding ring glinting in the overhead light. "Let's sit on the comfy seats. My back already hurts, but my new chair doesn't get delivered until Thursday."

Roxie headed for the couch and sat, crossing one knee with her boot. Her boss was former Army, so they'd bonded as much as friendly rivalry allowed.

"How are you?"

Roxie hadn't come up here for this. "I'm doing okay." She wasn't about to lie. "Are there any updates?"

"There was no evidence on the cardboard box, and nothing about the snake gave us a clue as to who sent it to you or where it came from." Clare shot her a sympathetic look. "One of your neighbors has a camera doorbell, but all it caught was a white delivery van. Nothing that we can pinpoint. So we need you to stay vigilant."

Roxie nodded. Not once had Clare doubted her story or asked her to prove Mark was—in fact—alive. "I will."

"We need you to go home and stay with Destiny."

Roxie flinched. "Why? She'll be in danger."

"She'll have a police presence since a whole group of officers volunteered for protection detail when they're not working. No one wants Blake's sister to get hurt. Same with you." Clare didn't waste a second. "And you need her."

"That's not a good reason to put her in danger."

"I'd argue the damage has already been done. So go be with your friend in your familiar comforting space. Live your life and let us take care of you."

Roxie pressed her lips together. Then she said, "Is that an order?"

"If you need it to be, yes." Clare nodded. "Go home, Roxie."

FOURTEEN

Liam pulled up outside Destiny's townhouse while on the phone with his lieutenant, Gage DeLuca. He shifted his truck into park, and his boss's voice came through the speakers. "You should have told them by now."

Liam let his hands fall to his lap. "I know. I want to get their next step set up so they have options."

"And yours?"

Liam said nothing. He was running out of avenues to go down with this.

"Do you know what you're going to do?"

"Intelligence doesn't need a sergeant right now." Liam had been too busy to make any other inquiries.

"There's a precinct on the north side of Benson that needs a new patrol sergeant. Want me to float your name, see what the chief thinks?"

Liam didn't have much choice. He had to move to whatever position remained open when his was closed as a full-time spot and transitioned to a collateral duty position.

"You'll still be the SWAT sergeant. I'll still be the SWAT command officer."

"Doesn't mean everything is going to be the same."

"I know this isn't about you," Gage said. "You want to make sure Blake and Jasper land somewhere they're good with, but you'll still get them on SWAT callouts."

"I know." Liam squeezed his eyes shut. "I don't know why I'm being a baby about it."

Gage chuckled. "That's fine because I do."

Liam opened his eyes and looked at the speaker. "And?"

"You'll figure it out. You've got enough to worry about right now."

"Did you get into that file?" Liam had looked up his father's case so he could convince Vanguard's Cold Case Department that looking into the OD of a homeless guy was a nothing sandwich. What he'd found was an Internal Affairs case number, which he didn't have authorization to open. Gage, however, was his lieutenant and had more clout as an officer.

"Not yet. I've punted it up the chain, but I don't anticipate it getting much response. I may skip a few steps and go talk to the commissioner."

"No one is gonna like it that you had Russ Franklin open a can of worms." The commissioner was a former US Marshal and, as a civilian position above the chief of police, he was effectively a liaison between the mayor who appointed him and the mayor's appointed chief over the department.

Better Gage than him. Despite the fact Jasper's dad was a state senator, Liam hated politics. Bureaucracy sucked. Climbing in rank only meant more glad-handing to get anything done. Give him old-fashioned, boots-on-the-ground work over political schmoozing any day.

Maybe that was the hang-up he had that Gage had figured out.

The front door opened, and Blake stepped out.

Liam said, "I've gotta go, Lieutenant. I'm on detail tonight."

"Stay safe." Gage hung up.

The lieutenant hadn't volunteered for protection detail, but he and his wife—Roxie's boss, Clare—were the first to be called if anything happened. They would be here within minutes.

Liam grabbed his backpack and a duffel of personal weapons since using department guns for a private op was a bad call. He had his off-duty pistol on his hip and strode up the front path to Blake. They shook, which ended up as a back-thumping hug.

"Thanks."

Liam nodded. "You've got that thing tonight."

"I should get to it. Leave you here." Blake shook hands with him. "Destiny knows what to do if anything happens. She's not working tonight, but she's got a test tomorrow morning, so she'll probably be studying."

"Copy that."

"Your job is to protect her from anything. Including Roxie, if that's the case."

Liam frowned.

"Jas told me what your buddy said about her. I don't think I need to be more worried than I am, but why should we care about this girl? She's gonna put my sister in danger." Blake didn't back down when a member of his family was threatened.

"She wouldn't hurt Destiny."

"I know." Blake huffed a laugh. "At Backdraft, she said she'd have killed my sister already if she was planning on it."

Liam blinked. "She's not going to hurt her. She's not like that." Great, now he was vouching for her—the woman currently at the window watching them through the blinds.

He was honestly surprised she was here. Or that both of them were. Maybe they wanted their familiar space, and it was easier to safeguard yourself if you noticed immediately something was wrong with your surroundings.

He pushed out a breath because her decision to stay here wasn't his business. He would be asking her about it if he got the chance, though. And with Destiny studying tonight that might happen. Quiet, alone time with Roxie.

Liam said, "Roxie would lay down her life for anyone facing a threat. For someone she cared about? You don't need to worry. She will do anything, including give her life, for your sister if that's what it comes down to."

Blake jingled the car keys in his hand. "So why does the military think she's unstable, possibly dangerous?"

"They never said she was dangerous. But they did recommend a psych eval." Liam's phone rang in his pocket. According to his watch, it wasn't his mom calling him back, so he ignored it. "She had one at the treatment center she attended, and they cleared her. The final was sent to the military, but it's not like we can read it. That means it's up to Roxie to tell us what we might need to know."

"I asked. She didn't volunteer the details." Blake lifted his brows. "But she did say she would tell you."

Liam pressed his lips together. He hadn't been able to figure out who the guy was that sent the snake. Someone she'd told him was dead. Right now, it made no sense, but he needed her to tell him if he was to have the intel that would keep her and Destiny safe.

And when did he start feeling the need to cover Roxie?

She'd lied to him. Misled him. Ditched him at the first chance. He shouldn't care one bit about her, but that fatal flaw in him that didn't let go when his heart got involved meant one thing—he had no chance to get out of this with his sanity intact.

"I'll check in later." Blake stepped by him.

"Copy that." Liam went to the front door and turned to scan the street just so he could catalog what vehicles and people were around. So he'd spot any changes that might be suspicious. Then he let himself in. "Destiny, it's Liam!"

"Living room!"

He headed there and found Destiny and Roxie beside each other, under a blanket with a bowl of popcorn between them.

Destiny waved to the chair. "You're just in time for the good part."

Liam spotted the chick flick on the TV and groaned. No wonder Blake had been ready to leave so fast, and it wasn't because he had a volunteer thing tonight coaching inner-city kids' basketball. "Great." He lowered himself into the chair.

"There's enchiladas on the stove," Roxie said. "Should be warm still."

Liam levered himself out of the chair and headed for the kitchen. He heard both women snicker, but it wasn't like this was a cowardly retreat. He was hungry, okay? He'd had a long day and lunch had been hours ago.

While he nuked the enchiladas a little just to make them piping hot, he texted his mom.

I REALLY NEED YOU TO CALL ME.

She might have zero intention of doing that, but his mom couldn't hide forever. They had dinner on Sundays every week that he could make it. As far as he knew, they were still on for this weekend. Sometimes Conrad and his family came, so they both got to see him and his wife and the girls. Not the time to talk about his dad's case. But Liam wasn't going to let this drop.

He needed to know why she'd hired Vanguard to reopen the case.

Liam took his plate and a fork and paper towel back to the living room and saw the TV again. He flinched.

Roxie smirked at him.

He shot her a look, and she burst out laughing. "It's not that bad."

As if she *wanted* to watch this. Knowing Destiny, this was about torturing both of them with too much sweet romance. It was practically thick in the air in this room.

"Welp, I have to study." Destiny jumped up from under the blanket.

Liam got a flash of the back of her knee, and she was gone.

"Gotta study!" Destiny's voice came from the hall.

Roxie started to laugh.

"There's nothing funny about this."

She only laughed harder, swiping a tear from her eye.

FIFTEEN

A second later, Roxie realized what she was doing and the awkwardness from teasing Liam hit home. She swallowed the laughter and reached for the popcorn bowl, scooping up what had spilled on the blanket and setting the bowl on Destiny's coffee table.

Liam had his plate on his knee. "It's good to see you laugh."

It was an odd posture, especially since she'd just been thinking how much of a guy he was for acting that way about a simple show on TV. "The movie wasn't that bad."

He lifted one brow, his fork almost to his mouth. "You liked it?"

"No, but it was what Destiny wanted to watch." Roxie grabbed the blanket, pulled her knees up, and held it to her front. As if the blanket would give her any kind of defense. It was more the feeling of being surrounded by comfort. Like strong arms—but none were available, and needing someone never ended well in her experience.

"You okay?"

"I never really know how to answer that."

Roxie turned off the TV. They'd always found a quiet place to be so they could talk. Why did people reach for a device or noise or a flashing screen rather than simply sitting? In the quiet, her mind could create its own ideas. So she could reason things out.

She wouldn't have realized what Mark had planned without it. Instead, she'd have lived in oblivion and probably would have died there, because it was easier than turning the tide.

The whole thing made her heart hurt for anyone in a situation that caused fear, a situation where they felt trapped.

Liam set his plate on the table. "I figure you're either all right, or you're not. What's so hard about that?"

He wasn't being mean. She'd always appreciated the pragmatic view of the world he had. The way so much was black or white for him. Cops needed that, or things got cloudy really fast. Roxie had to push out a long breath, lean her head against the couch.

"I can make myself scarce if you need to rest."

She shook her head. "I'm okay." Which meant she'd just invited him to sit and talk with her. Was that what she wanted? It would only make things more complicated. "I just haven't been at peace in a long time."

"Depends where you get your peace from. But the person I talk to about that is my mom, and she's currently not replying to any of my messages." He sat back in his chair, one boot on the other knee. "But peace isn't that far away. All you have to do is reach out and grab it."

"Destiny had me pray with her. I don't know what good it did." Faith, or God, felt so far away. Mark was here, but no one believed her.

No way did she want to risk Liam not believing her. That

would hurt far too much. She'd always respected his opinion way more than anyone else's.

Roxie shook her head. "I don't know how I feel about any of that church stuff. I know you go—"

"It's been a while."

She wasn't entirely surprised about that, given he seemed so much...harder...these days. "But it's like everyone around me believes, and they want me to be interested."

"No pressure from me. Believe what you want."

She shot him a look.

"It's important, and I want you to. Don't get me wrong." He lifted his fingers. "But I get the feeling you don't want to be pressured or told what to think."

"I definitely don't want that." Roxie looked around. "Being here... You probably think I shouldn't be putting Destiny in danger, but Clare ordered me to be here."

Liam pointed up at the corner of the wall where it met the ceiling. "I'm guessing that might play into the reason why."

"Cameras?"

"My guess is Vanguard wired up the whole place after the snake thing."

Roxie shuddered. "Makes sense. I should be mad because that feels a whole lot like being controlled."

"Call it strategic protection. Two people to safeguard. It makes sense if they're together. Assuming they aren't going to try to kill each other." He flashed a smile.

"Has that happened?"

He chuckled. "Protective custody. They said they were in love, and they were going to flip on their dealer who was about to meet with the drug supplier. So we take them both to a motel and take shifts. Two in the morning, they start tearing up the room. She's throwing lamps. He gets the shower curtain off the rail, puts a hole in the wall in the process, and then he takes the plastic sheet and tries to suffocate her to death. It was nuts."

Roxie blinked, almost laughing, even though it was tragically not funny at all. "Wow."

"Yeah." Liam chuckled.

They lapsed into silence, the comfortable kind that two old friends settle into. Roxie soaked up that moment of peace, even knowing she didn't have the kind of peace that sank in her soul. Situational peace was all she could have, it seemed, and she enjoyed that when she felt it tangibly. Like right now —with Liam.

"Thanks for coming over."

Liam gave her a soft smile she really liked. "Destiny is a great kid. I was happy to pitch in."

He might've known she would be here, or maybe he hadn't. She couldn't get a read on how he felt about that either.

"If we're going to protect her adequately, I need to know the threat."

He'd finally brought it up. She should be prepared.

He continued, "I need you to tell me who sent you the snake, Rox."

Oh, boy. She liked him saying her name like that. So much it could get a little intoxicating hearing it. She gave herself a second, then said, "You didn't call around and ask about me today?"

"I want to hear what's important from you."

Because he didn't like what he'd heard, and he still trusted her enough to tell him the truth. But could she? Could she say that name out loud? She'd held it in for so long, as if speaking it aloud would conjure him. But he wasn't an evil spirit. Just a man.

Still, to have Liam look at her the way everyone else from the Marines had?

She couldn't handle that.

He spoke again, and she braced herself, but he said, "Like why you finished Search and Rescue dog handler training, but you aren't a dog handler for Search and Rescue? Unless you're on call. But I don't see a dog."

She was already nodding before he had even finished, a slow acknowledgment. "I was doing great." She sucked in a breath through her nose. "The dog I was working with was great, nothing wrong with him, but we didn't bond like I thought we should. We never would've been in sync in that instinctive way I thought we should."

"So it's about a dog?"

Yes, it was. Her heart squeezed in her chest. "Seeing Maverick get hurt. Watching Mitchell and Tessa panic because River was hurt as well, and they couldn't help both." She squeezed her eyes shut. "It reminded me too much of—" Her voice broke.

She heard him get up, then felt the depression of the cushion as he sat beside her. Then his soft voice said, "Harley?"

She'd told him years ago.

Roxie sucked in a shuddering breath. "I couldn't go through that again. I thought I was fine. It never even occurred to me that putting a dog in danger would end up making me flash back to Harley."

"We're supposed to be cut up from our time overseas."

"And yet I'm far more traumatized because my high school boyfriend got mad and ended up hitting my dog with his truck as he drove away in a huff." She pulled in more air. "The worst part is that I didn't even think about it."

"Getting blindsided is the worst."

"Happened in Vanguard training. We were clearing rooms, and I got boxed in. They used flash bangs, and the ringing in my ears, plus the smell." She glanced over. "I froze."

"Happens to the best of us."

As if it had ever happened to him. "I'm not supposed to be a mess. I'm supposed to be strong—body and mind. Not ready to fall apart at any second."

SIXTEEN

Liam stared at her. Clearly she didn't see him in the same light—as someone ready to fall apart at any second—which just proved how well he'd managed to hide things.

Listening to her, watching the look in her eyes—the fear and the pain so close to the surface—made him want to pull her close. Enough so that he'd moved to sit by her. Now he kept his hands to himself and didn't tug her against him, despite what seemed like an ever-present ache to do so. But no. He couldn't open his heart again like this.

Ongoing consensus from the military was that she'd lost it somehow. But how was that fair? She hadn't had a breakdown. This was real fear for a good reason. The haunted look in her eyes was evidence enough. But he needed to stick to the facts, not the gut-level attraction that drew him close to her.

Or the way she'd let him lean on her when he found out his father had died.

He wasn't ever going to forget that memory, and with her here, it was far too tempting to add similar memories to that one.

They needed to talk, or he was going to get lost in his head.

"One day, you're going to fall in love with a dog again." He'd wanted to get one himself, but his work schedule made that difficult. And yet, his need for companionship might just win out. "I know you will."

"What if I don't want to because I'm too scared?" She picked at the blanket. "If something happens, I'll be destroyed all over again. That's why I bailed on dog handling. Because I'm not strong enough."

"You have no clue how strong you are, Rox." He reached over and covered her hand with his. "You were strong for me when I had nothing and needed to hold on to something." He forced himself to squeeze her hand gently and then let go.

She didn't flat out disagree with him, but she didn't necessarily agree either.

Actually, that wasn't a bad idea. Maybe the K-9 division needed a sergeant.

"We don't know what the future is going to hold." Might as well break his news. She was about the only person he could tell without it being something that affected her as well. "They're disbanding the full-time SWAT team in Benson. My lieutenant already got shifted over to float between departments. He'll have a command soon, probably with narcotics or robbery homicide. We're down to three guys, and we should be adding more, but instead they decided to cut the budget and put us all in different departments until we're called out together."

"Breaking up the band."

"It's been more like a family." A lump rose in his throat. "One I didn't know I needed."

With one brother in Alaska and the other busy with his family, that left his mom. Not the same as having his dad here as well. He'd needed the brotherhood of SWAT after leaving the Marine Corps, which had felt like he'd had a limb cut off.

"You're worried about Blake and Jasper?"

"They'll be fine." He blew out a breath and shook his head. "I need to tell them, though. It's not fair to hide it any longer when they should be answering calls about open positions. I don't know why I can't just say it out loud."

"Because it hurts."

It really did. "I liked what we had, but then Dakota got in trouble with pain meds. We had to suffer through losing him. Gage—Lieutenant DeLuca—met Clare, and that wasn't easy for them, but they have each other now."

"She's great." Roxie smiled. "I love them together."

Liam did as well. "They... They just fit in a way that's unbelievable." And it made him want the same thing.

For years, he'd assumed that would be with Anne—Roxie. Then it had all fallen apart. He'd lost faith in almost everything, what with losing his dad the way he had and then losing her. He'd been struggling with faith ever since, figuring God probably forgot about him as well. Why else would it seem like He hadn't given Liam anything he wanted?

Even though his Christian life wasn't all about what God could give him, he'd been waiting for God's plan to show up for far too long.

"I need that." She exhaled a sigh. "With a dog. But I'm going to outlive it, so even if it grows to old age, I still have to lose it eventually."

Liam scratched his chin and tried not to laugh. He'd been thinking about waiting for God to bring him the love he wanted in a wife, and she was thinking about a dog? He nearly chuckled aloud. He managed to say, "No one says you have to have a dog of your own. You could still work with Mitchell's, right? Work with the dogs but not take one home.

Or volunteer with dogs. Be a foster dog mom, or a dog sitter on that app where you watch dogs while people are on vacation. There are lots of options."

"I can't do a lot of those things. Not with my life the way it is right now." She swallowed. "I don't like it when they're in danger. I can't put a dog through that."

"But with Mitchell's training center, it's like having a company car versus your own vehicle, right?"

She frowned at him. "Sure, except that it's a living being that requires care and attention."

He shrugged, just trying to lighten the mood. "I like my truck."

Roxie rolled her eyes so hard she was going to give herself a headache. How could he get her to tell him who it was that had sent the snake? He couldn't protect her if he had no idea of the threat level. Knowing who it was meant he'd be able to assess that person's skills. The fact that no one in the military was prepared to bend a little and give him what he needed wasn't a bad thing—it was correct in terms of protecting her privacy.

But he didn't like being in the dark.

Roxie said, "I should go see Mitchell. I never really explained why I didn't come back after I finished training. And I haven't returned any of Tessa's calls." She winced. "I've been a bad friend. They did a lot to help me with..." She caught herself and stopped talking.

Liam pressed his lips together rather than jump on that. She seemed so skittish sometimes, then strong a second later. He had to tread carefully. "I'd like to know what happened."

"I know."

"Not just so I can protect you." She had to know there was more to it than that. "But because you're here for a reason, same as me."

"To protect Destiny?"

Of course, she'd like to think that, but he shook his head. "You know it's not that. It's us."

"Because it's always been us." She sounded almost broken. She shifted on the couch and turned to him. "And then it turned bad, like everything in my life."

That's what she thought? "Roxie—"

"Don't." She shook her head, looking away. "It's done. It doesn't matter anymore." She got up, grabbed his plate, and headed for the kitchen.

Liam gave her a moment in case that was what she needed. He leaned his head back on the seat. *I got pretty far off track, didn't I?* He needed to crack open his Bible when he got home—after he dusted off the thing.

Maybe he'd discover what Gage meant when he said he'd figured out why Liam couldn't let go. Possibly because his job was all he had. And he *liked* working with SWAT. Feeling like a squad of brothers doing good in Benson.

His phone vibrated in his pocket. Liam shifted enough to slide it out and saw Karina's name on the screen. "O'Connell."

She gasped. "Someone is breaking into my house."

He shot up off the couch, then realized why he was here. "I have to get cover here where I am. Then I'll be right there. I'll have a car come to you, okay?"

"I-I think they're coming."

"Hide. The bathroom. The closet. Get somewhere and stay small and quiet." He headed for the hall, aware that Roxie had come over from the kitchen. "I'll be there. Okay?"

"Hurry."

He hung up and got on the phone again and called dispatch for a car to Karina's. Then he called Jasper. "Jas, I need cover at Destiny's."

"Six minutes."

"Copy that." Liam hung up.

"I'll go with you."

Liam glanced over, about to tell her no, but the words didn't come out.

"I'll tell Destiny we're leaving and that Jasper is coming over to stay with her." Roxie trailed off down the hall.

His phone buzzed. A car was on its way to Karina's house.

He prayed they got there in time.

SEVENTEEN

Liam pulled up in his truck outside a tiny home in an older neighborhood. Not rough, just established with an air of "too busy working to worry about the yard." Roxie twisted her hands together. She probably shouldn't be here, what with the cops and Liam doing this in an official capacity. Or perhaps he wasn't, since he was technically off duty.

He hadn't told her no, so maybe he wanted her here. If it was so she could support him, then that was what she would do. Bonus, Destiny was protected and being away from Roxie could save her from being a target. Roxie still didn't know why Clare insisted that she be there.

It was probably what Liam had said about it being easier to protect two people if they were in the same place.

Or Clare had such a big slice of empathy in her that she knew Roxie wasn't going to be okay alone. Yet another way Roxie should be strong and came up short.

But right now, this wasn't about her. It was about Liam. So she turned to him. "I'll hang back. Let you talk to the officers and see Karina."

"Stay close by. Just in case."

He wanted to protect her while they were out. Even at a scene where someone he cared about—the woman he'd been having dinner with, actually—was in danger, and he was still conscientious enough to make sure she was safe.

"I will." Roxie got out but stuck close to the officer.

Near enough to hear the guy say, "House is empty. Signs of forced entry."

Liam stared at the structure. "I'll take a look."

"Suit yourself." The officer waved at the house. "I'll call for crime scene techs if you have reason to believe the resident has been kidnapped. We can loop in the FBI as well."

This guy didn't seem to feel like he was being second-guessed. Maybe the community of law enforcement in Benson was better than that. Close. A team. At least Liam had that. She was gaining it with Vanguard, but even still, it would take time.

A crowd of people had gathered down the street. More than one officer had taken someone aside, talking to them and writing in a notebook.

"Roxie?"

She pushed off the car and followed Liam to the front door. The officer gave her an odd frown. She flashed her Vanguard ID just in case that settled things. Often, it did in Benson since the CEO had married one of the PD lieutenants.

Liam entered the house.

"Not sure I'm supposed to be inside the residence." She stepped in behind him.

"Let's do a walk through. I want your impression."

"Because we worked so many missing persons' cases in Afghanistan?"

Liam didn't look at her, he scanned the entryway. "You

know what a fight looks like. What the aftermath looks like, right?"

It was an odd question with a leading tone. "Are you using whatever happened with this woman to find out more about me, as in, I'll be so empathetic, I'll say too much?"

"I multitask. And you're safer next to me."

"He's not going to jump out of the shadows and shoot me. Or shoot me without ever leaving the shadows." If that were the case, she'd have set up to shoot him first. Fair was only fair. "Now let's figure out what happened to your friend."

Liam kept looking, and she stuck with him, searching the area around where he was also so they didn't miss anything.

"She's the sister of a CI of mine. And it's looking like she was dragged into the same thing her sister was trying to get out of."

"With the Russians?"

Liam nodded, opening the closet doors in the bedroom. "Possibly. And it got her sister killed. But she said she wanted nothing to do with them."

"Maybe that's the problem." Roxie lowered herself to look under the bed. "Phone. Your side." She lifted up to kneeling and motioned. "Under the skirt."

The device looked like it had slid under the bed. Or been placed there to hide it.

Liam took a look. "That isn't her phone. And we need crime scene techs to handle it."

Roxie let out a sigh. "I don't think I'd make a good cop. I don't like rules that much, I feel like they were made to be broken."

Liam looked up from his own phone and smiled. "Rules keep us safe."

She sucked in a breath at the words Mark had drilled into her. His rules, of course.

He frowned. "Roxie?"

"I don't like rules." She got up and headed out, moving through the house to look at the empty kitchen and dining area. The back door was open.

"Hey."

She glanced back at Liam. "Maybe she left? Or was dragged out?"

He nodded, a soft look on his face. "Tell me who sent you that snake?"

She sucked in a sharp breath. "I need to go outside." She started to move by him, but Liam caught her arm. "I need air."

"Don't walk away from this. Let me help you."

"I need to do this myself, or I'll give away the will and the strength I have *again*. If I let you fix the problem, then I'll never learn how to stand up on my own."

They stood there, staring at each other.

One of the officers cleared his throat.

Liam spun around. "Hey, Gutierrez."

"Crime scene techs should be here in ten. Find anything?"

"A phone that isn't Karina's. So we need that processed first."

The officer lifted his chin, then left. Roxie used Liam's diverted attention to step by him and fast-walk after the cop to the front door. She shouldn't have offered to come here with Liam. She should have stayed with Destiny and the police officer protecting her.

But it was Liam.

Because it's always been us.

But she'd thought he would come and find her, and he hadn't. Maybe even part of her had dreamed far too much that he might show up and realize what had happened to her. That he might save her.

But he never did.

She strode to his truck and set her palms on the warm hood. Just long enough to take a few minutes and try and find that peace on her own, the same feeling she'd immersed herself in on the couch with him. Now it was gone.

Evaporated.

A warm hand touched her shoulder blade, and she spotted his boots beside hers. "Why don't you take my truck back to Destiny's? I need to stay here and see what's on that phone. You can go get some rest. It's late."

She straightened, and he offered her his keys.

"Keep your eyes open." He dropped the keys into her hand. "Do you want an officer escort?"

She shook her head. "I've got my gun if I need it."

He looked like he wanted to say more. Probably they would both agree now that she shouldn't have come. Much like in the Marines, their feelings were at war with duty and where their focus should be. Another case of bad timing.

She and Liam were never going to have anything between them.

"Have a good night." She stepped back from him and climbed in, pulling out without looking at him.

What was the point? Any hope of a relationship was dead on arrival.

She turned up the music loud, humming to the radio to tune out the clamor of her thoughts. Why dwell on the sad enormity of her life? Maybe she should give faith and Christianity a go. Honestly, could it make her life any worse?

It might even make it better, and right now, she could use at least one positive thing. Destiny said God had brought them together as friends. Maybe that was true. And maybe knowing Him would be more of that easy warm connection she had with her roommate.

Lights flashed in her rearview.

Before she could get a clear idea of who was behind her, the vehicle slammed into the back of Liam's truck.

Roxie yelped. She gripped the wheel and held the truck steady. Phone. She needed her phone.

She pulled back the Velcro over her right leg pocket and grabbed the phone.

The vehicle behind revved and slammed into her again. Her hand hit the volume knob, shooting the music up to earsplitting levels. The phone hit the floor on the passenger side.

Her front right wheel clipped the curb, and she jerked the wheel to the left. She swiped a parked car but got control back. The vehicle behind had to be a bigger truck. It made contact again, but in the dark, she couldn't make anything out.

She needed to pull over. Get out of the way of people in other vehicles.

There. A parking lot.

Roxie jerked the wheel hard to the right, bumping the curb into the parking lot of a flooring company.

The vehicle behind slammed into the back corner. She lost control, barreling into the front window with the brakes screeching. Glass shattered.

The air bag deployed in her face.

EIGHTEEN

"What about any of the neighbors? Did they see a vehicle leave?" Liam stood just outside the front door, facing the two officers who had been interviewing neighbors.

Both shook their heads. "Nothing. What did she say to you?"

He reiterated the brief conversation with Karina before he'd called it in and then asked Jasper to cover Destiny. "I told her to find a closet or hide in the bathroom."

"Maybe she did, but someone dragged her out."

Liam scratched his jaw. This was all wrong. She hadn't liked that her sister Veronika was informing on the Russians she worked for, giving Liam shipping information and details of financial transactions she recorded as their office manager. Karina liked it less when the whole thing got her sister killed.

Murdered in her home.

And Liam hadn't found the person who'd done it.

Was that what had happened here? Karina's attempt to solve her sister's murder had gone wrong? Was she getting close to dangerous people, trying to get information?

The crime scene tech stepped out of the house. She'd gone in with all her things—and a laptop. Wearing booties and a medical grade mask, now hanging around her neck, she'd already gone through a box of gloves since each piece of evidence had to be handled with a new pair of gloves. "Sarge?"

He twisted around. "The phone?"

"Definitely a burner. Just a few messages and a half dozen pictures. You're going to want to take a look—I've already sent them to your email."

"Thanks."

She disappeared back into the house. Liam pulled out his phone and opened the email from her, which included a link to the PD server. He scrolled through the images first, spotting a scene from a local club with Karina drinking and partying beside Raphi Obolensky.

His jaw clenched.

In another one, she was by a pool, somewhere with palm trees. Still with Raphi, a few of his men in the background. "She's dating him."

Gutierrez looked over his shoulder. "So are about six other women near as I've been able to put together."

Liam glanced over.

Gutierrez shrugged. "After Nico killed that guy in holding, everyone has had eyes out for his brother. Looking for a legitimate reason to stop him or even bring him in."

"And he has more than one woman?"

"Guys like that always do. But there's a bartender at the Last Sip, and she's pretty sure he'll propose soon."

"Hmm." That was good work. "Who is your captain? I may have you sit in a meeting. You might be able to add information we aren't aware of."

It did seem like this whole situation could use a taskforce.

Light sparked in the officer's expression. "Thanks, Sarge. That'd be great." Gutierrez said, "Is what was on the phone enough for a warrant? Maybe Raphi is the one who came here and took her."

It would be simpler if he were. "It's just circumstantial. Unless one of your witnesses saw him drag her out, we have nothing to tie them together. Even an argument between them in the last few days isn't enough. The prosecutor will want more than that to get a judge to sign off on any run at Obolensky we make. And a guy like that is slippery. If he gets wind we're after him he'll lock his stuff down tight so we never find anything."

Gutierrez made a face.

Liam nearly chuckled. "Makes you want to take the detective exam, doesn't it?"

Gutierrez grinned.

The officer with him said, "Just sounds like a lot of paperwork."

Liam nodded, since the guy wasn't wrong. He was about to break off and go into the house to see if crime scene had found anything else when the other officer said, "Sarge?"

"Yeah?" Liam didn't know this guy, but his name badge read "Allman."

"That woman you were with, the one that works for Vanguard?" A different light shone in this guy's eyes. "Is she... seeing anyone?"

Liam stared at the guy for a long second. Then he turned and stepped into the house.

Behind him, he heard a yelp, and then someone said, "Idiot."

Liam found the crime scene tech. Before he could say anything, his phone rang. "One sec."

The tech nodded and got back to work. Since she probably wanted to get on with her job and not be here all night *and* into tomorrow processing the scene.

Liam stepped back into the hall and frowned at the number on the screen. Not one of his saved contacts. "Sergeant O'Connell."

"Liam O'Connell?"

"Yes."

"The registered owner of a red Ford." The person listed his truck model and license plate number.

"That's me."

"I'm calling from Pro-Tec. Your vehicle's GPS system alerted us to a crash, and we're confirming whether you require assistance at this time."

Cold ran through him. "I wasn't the one driving." He turned and strode to the door and then out. "I need a ride." He motioned to Gutierrez.

The officer whirled and started to jog to a patrol car.

"Do you know anything about what happened?" Liam got in the passenger side, gripping the phone while he buckled up.

"We have your vehicle's location."

Liam put the call on speaker.

The dispatcher said, "I take it you aren't the driver currently."

He'd read that right. "A friend borrowed it. I need the location. I'm a Benson PD officer, and I'm dispatching to the location." *Roxie.* Was she hurt? They needed to get there *now* and find out.

"We have police and ambulance on their way already."

"Great." Liam tried to let go of some of his tension. "Tell me where to go."

He had to give his badge number, but the dispatcher told them the address. Gutierrez flipped on lights and sirens and headed there. Liam gripped his phone and ran his hand down his pant leg over his knee to get rid of some of the sweat. *Roxie.* He'd let her go alone, and now she'd crashed?

"Almost there."

Yeah, Gutierrez would go far in the department. A good guy plus a solid cop equaled a stellar combination.

He pulled into a parking lot and Liam got a look at his truck on the far side of an ambulance. A fire truck currently battled a fire in the flooring warehouse store she'd crashed into. *Roxie.* He shoved the door open and ran to the scene commander. "Did you get the driver out?"

"Sergeant." The fire captain lifted his chin. "We're working on locating her."

Liam frowned. "What do you mean? She was driving."

The captain nodded. "I know. But the front seat was empty when we got here."

Everything in Liam tensed. Where was Roxie? If she'd been taken like Karina... He sucked in a breath.

"One of my guys recognized it as your truck. We figured it was you. If you give us the driver's name and a description, we can direct our search."

"I'll help."

Gutierrez set a hand on his shoulder. "Sarge—"

He shrugged it off. "I'll help."

The captain said, "You don't go into that building."

"Good. I'll search outside." She could be out here somewhere. They had her description now, so they'd be able to ID her.

Liam set off, walking around the building and scanning the parking lot. Behind the building was a row of fencing overgrown with a hedge. Not a great place to hide if that had become necessary. He didn't have her number to call it. He could get ahold of Gage, and have Clare give him Roxie's number. He'd have to admit he hadn't asked for it, but the chance to save her would be worth it.

Where is she, Lord?

He passed a massive dumpster and checked the far side. Pulled up short. He turned back to Gutierrez. "Go tell the captain I got her. And have EMS get back here."

"On it, Sarge." The officer jogged away, his belt jingling with each footfall.

Liam approached her slowly, eyeing the gun in her hands. The one Gutierrez hadn't seen. Liam stayed out of the line of fire. "Roxie, it's okay. You're safe." He took a couple of steps toward her. "You're safe now."

She didn't even blink, just sat huddled against the wall and the side of the trash bin. That gun in her hands.

He crouched beside her and laid his hand on top of the gun. "Let go of the gun, Roxie. Give it to me."

"I can't let go."

"Yes, you can." For some reason he couldn't explain, Liam said, "Let go. I'll catch you."

NINETEEN

A garage door rolled up, one in a row of doors. Clare's car was parked in a spot across from them. She and Gage had shown up at the crash scene and given Liam a set of keys. He'd left her no choice but to go with them after she'd told the officer what she could.

Liam pulled the borrowed car into a garage at the back of a house Roxie had never been to. The car stopped, and she jerked with the motion but couldn't make her limbs move. He'd taken her gun. All she could see when she closed her eyes was Mark standing over her.

His words rang in her mind.

The door to the house opened, and Gage and Clare stepped out. Liam met them at the hood of the truck.

She flinched, then realized he stood beside her.

"You're out of it." He leaned in and slid an arm under her knees. "Come on."

She should argue that she could walk, but the words wouldn't form. She managed to lift a hand and grasp the collar of his SWAT T-shirt. Her head swam as he moved through the house and sat her on a couch. She curled her knees up.

Clare handed her a mug. "Hold this. Drink it slowly."

The stoneware radiated heat into her fingers. She took a sip of the strong tea, sweet and rich. Not a blend she usually liked, which served to jolt her thoughts together rather than let her sink deeper into oblivion.

You're stronger than this.

You have to be.

Gage sat in the armchair to her right. Clare sat on the arm of that chair, close to her husband.

Liam sat beside her on the couch, but not close enough they could reach out easily. "What happened?"

"I was run off the road."

"In my truck?"

She winced. "The other vehicle was big. I don't know what it was. I never saw. It was too dark." All she'd seen were headlights in the rearview. "The lights were really bright. They rammed the back of your truck a couple of times."

"I know that," Liam said. "It's what you told the officer. Now tell me what you didn't say. Like how you ended up around the back of the building."

How was she supposed to tell him it was instinct? More than likely, nothing but a trauma reaction. For a moment, she'd been back in that car with Mark, back on that night when it was all supposed to end.

Roxie lifted one hand and traced the scar on her temple. "I think I shoved the door open."

She set the mug down and looked at her stinging palms. She had grazes on her arms she hadn't noticed. She'd refused medical attention because who wanted to be poked and prodded when they were trying valiantly to hold it together?

"I know I fell out." She rubbed her hands together. Thankfully, she hadn't broken skin. "I think I ran through the building, out the back door. The alarm was going off."

"Why didn't you stay in the truck and wait for help?" Liam shifted.

His curious expression made it clear he was trying to understand. But how could he?

Did he know what it felt like to be completely and utterly helpless? Terrified out of his mind?

Clare said, "When did you see him?"

"In the back. Outside."

"You should've stayed in the truck." Liam fisted his hands on his knees.

Everything in Roxie tensed. "I couldn't form a thought or come up with a word. I wouldn't have even been able to tell you my name. I didn't have the judgment needed to conclude it was better to stay in truck, Lee."

He only stared at her.

Gage said, "You were having a panic attack."

She didn't know Clare's husband well. His dark features might seem threatening to some, but she saw understanding in his eyes and managed to nod.

"You fled the truck because that was what instinct told you to do."

Roxie looked from Gage to her boss, who knew the whole story. "I had to get out. There was nothing else I could've done in that moment except get somewhere away from there."

Liam sighed, so she took a break from Gage's and Clare's obvious sympathy for her situation and glanced at him. He said, "What happened between your going outside and me finding you?"

She remembered him grabbing her gun. "Did you take my weapon?"

He nodded. "You can have it back." But he didn't give it to her now. "After you tell me all of it."

"He was there." She grabbed the tea and took another

drink of the bracing liquid. Enough to jog more words loose. "He stood over me, and he laughed." Roxie ran her hands along her arms, rubbing some warmth into her limbs. "He said it wasn't time yet, but he would kill me. After he destroyed everything."

"Who?"

She couldn't put it off any longer. "Mark Mills."

Liam flinched. "I was at his funeral. He burned to death in a car accident, drove his vehicle off a cliff or something. He's dead."

Clare hissed a breath. Gage ran a hand through his hair.

Liam said, "I watched his family grieve for him. It was real. They buried a body in that grave."

That part Roxie hadn't been able to figure out. Unless he'd had a body in the trunk of the car, but given what she'd seen? "I thought I saw him burn. I thought he was dead. But he's *here*."

Liam didn't believe her. Sometimes she didn't even believe herself. But Clare hadn't questioned it. Since none of them believed she was being haunted by a ghost, because that would be bizarre, there had to be a real, flesh-and-blood explanation.

"I've gone over the coroner's files, the police reports, and the evidence they collected," Clare said. "As far as the world is concerned, Mark Mills is dead." She paused for a second, then continued, "But if Roxie believes Mark is alive, then he is. Or there's another reasonable explanation."

Liam frowned. "He didn't rise from the dead." He glanced at her. "You said you saw him burn."

Her stomach flipped over. "I was in the car when it went over the cliff. Mark and I..." She took a breath. "It was good at first. Then it wasn't. I was going to leave him, and he didn't want that. He would've killed us both."

"No one ever said anything about a second passenger," Clare said. "It's a miracle you managed to keep it quiet that you were there. And it's a miracle you managed to get out of that situation alive."

Roxie brushed hair back from her face, right by the scar. "I crawled far enough away that no one came to look. I blacked out a couple of times but managed to get to a road. I hitchhiked with a family who let me use their first aid kit, and they dropped me at a medical center. I think I freaked out the kids."

Liam just stared at her.

"Four days in the hospital. I told them I fell hiking, and that I was going to call my mom. I pretended I was being picked up and just left. Took a bus. Kept moving. I didn't want anyone asking me about the crash. I couldn't talk about Mark. I didn't even want to think about him. It was my fresh start. Nothing but blue skies and drinks with umbrellas. I hitched up the Oregon coast for a while. Took some odd jobs, made some money. Tried to figure out what I wanted to do." She swallowed.

"That's when you started to see him?" Clare asked.

It had seemed unbelievable at first. Being haunted by a ghost. "I contacted a hacker I knew years ago to get his financials. After his 'death' his credit card was used in towns I'd been to. His phone called whatever motel room I was staying in, and he was on the line just breathing. I started to see him on the street. I got fired from a couple of jobs because I was losing it. Seeing things."

Clare said, "I'd hoped you would have some time to rest. Get some peace. But it seems like he's escalating. Getting closer to you, which will end up with a confrontation. So for now, you'll be staying in the safe house apartment in the Vanguard building."

"Don't trap me there." She shook her head. "I can choose to stay somewhere I'm safe, but then I need to work. Don't lock me down, I'll go crazy." She gasped. "I need to end this. Not hide." She grabbed the sides of her head, two handfuls of hair. "I feel like I'm going crazy. I'm not here to confront him. I came here to expose him, to expose what he did to his first wife so people will believe me. It was a good plan." She looked at Clare.

Her boss nodded, empathy on her face. "I have a friend who narrowed down the search area. They're looking for her remains."

Roxie's heart sank. "Tessa?"

The K-9 handler for Search and Rescue in Benson was the only person Roxie knew with a cadaver-trained dog. Would Tessa really find Mark's first wife's remains? Clare hadn't even told her she was working it.

Her boss nodded. "I gave you other assignments, so I figured I'd help you with yours."

Tears filled Roxie's eyes.

"That's what friends do."

TWENTY

Liam kicked off his shoes in the front hall, his head full of her story.

Roxie was in his kitchen. In his house. For now.

Clare and Gage had left, promising to check in first thing. Liam should take Roxie back to Destiny's place so she could have her freedom—and her things. After they'd had some time here and she'd rested would be good.

Wherever she stayed he would ensure she was protected. He'd sit in Gage's car that he'd borrowed outside on the curb all night. Just to be safe.

She'd come to Benson trying to solve a case—Mark's first wife's disappearance. The guy had told Liam about how his wife ran off with another guy while he was deployed. Liam had always thought there was something off about the lance corporal. He'd never liked the way Mark looked at Roxie, but it hadn't been anything dangerous.

She'd fallen for him after she got out?

And after she and Liam had that unspoken pact agreeing to give it a shot if they got the chance. The Marine Corps regulations had kept them from getting personal with a relationship. When his tour came to an end, he'd left to come back to Benson.

She'd left...and fallen into Mark's arms.

It didn't make sense to him, but that wasn't the point. It was her life, and she'd made a choice—whatever the situation had been. She'd told them she wanted out of the relationship. Mark had forced it and nearly killed her.

If it wasn't Mark terrorizing her now, then who was it? And why did she believe that person was Mark?

Right now, he had to bury his own hurt and figure out how to help her. On top of that, Karina was missing. He needed to get to work tomorrow and pick up the search from the night shift detectives to figure out where she'd gone, if they didn't locate her overnight. He couldn't be in charge of the case, given their personal connection, but he could do everything in his power to help.

He headed for the kitchen and stopped in the doorway. Roxie stood at the sink, running her hands under the water. He waited to see if she'd do it herself, then went over and turned the water off. He tugged the towel off the front of the oven where his mom had put it the last time she was here and dried off her hands.

She shuddered. "It was him."

She thought he didn't believe her.

Liam took the towel and tossed it on the counter. Then he tugged her against him and wrapped his arms around her. She stiffened but, after a second, wrapped her arms around his waist and held on. He'd ditched his gun belt, so there wasn't a bunch of stuff between them.

Unfortunately, that meant she fit perfectly there. This was dangerous territory. She wasn't in the right mental place to deal with him coming on to her, so he'd need to keep some distance.

"When you're ready, I'll take you back to Destiny's."

Her arms tightened reflexively.

"Or you can borrow a shirt, and I'll sleep on the couch." Those were the only two options he was prepared to offer. Given her history, she probably wouldn't opt to stay.

"I want to stay here." She spoke against his shirt.

Liam rested his chin on the top of her head. "Okay."

He could barely wrap his mind around this. Mark was dead—Liam had been at the funeral. Now she was saying Mark was alive? She was investigating his wife's disappearance like it was a death.

Tomorrow he'd have to go back to work and trust Vanguard, and Clare, to have her back. Help her solve her problem. For now, though, he could be there for her.

"I should call Tessa."

He shifted. "Right now?"

She blew out a breath. "Probably tomorrow." She eased back in his arms. "I have no idea where my phone is."

"The officer gave it to me from the truck. They were surprised when the vehicle was empty, but I'm glad you're okay." He ran his thumb down the scar on the side of her head.

She closed her eyes.

Liam leaned down and rested his forehead against hers. It might be a miracle she was alive, but there was still a whole series of hurdles between them. "I called you."

She jerked back. "After I left the house?"

He shook his head. "Not tonight. Years ago. Actually, about six months before Mark's funeral."

Her expression shuttered. "I never saw it."

"You didn't pick up. I got a text reply saying not to call again. You didn't want to see me, ever."

Her eyes closed. "That wasn't me."

Liam's heart broke all over again—the way it had when he'd read that text.

"I thought you'd moved on." And she had, but not in the way either of them thought. If the end of the relationship was anything like the rest of it, who knew what Mark had subjected her to? She could have ended up like his first wife, missing with no one having a clue where she'd ended up. With a cadaver dog looking for her.

His whole body shuddered. *I'd have lost you.*

Tears ran down her cheeks.

He reached for her again. "Please don't cry."

She waved him off, swiping at her cheeks. "Why not? It's so sad it's tragic. Kind of like everything else in my life right now."

"What are you talking about?" Liam asked. "Vanguard has your back. You and Destiny are close. I'm here, and I'll do whatever I can to help."

"That's why I need to call Tessa. She's been helping me out, and what have I been doing? Ignoring her." Roxie winced. "I can't believe she's doing that for Vanguard. For me. I don't want to be that person, a bad friend. Or a weak woman who falls for a line and gets sucked into a situation that ends with the smell of burning flesh and blood all over my face." The hollow expression in her eyes rocked him to his core.

Now that she'd opened up more was starting to emerge. Because she trusted him?

Liam leaned his hips back against the counter. "You're exhausted. We both need rest." They could talk all night, and it might be good for both of them to get a lot of things out. But she didn't need to sit in the sadness over their missed opportunity. Tonight he'd rather focus on what might be.

Another miracle. One that gave them a future, and a hope.

She let out a long sigh and nodded. "Thanks."

"For what?"

"I don't think I could've handled it if it was anyone but you who found me behind the building. It would have been a lot harder." She lifted her gaze from her hands. "You make things easier."

"That's a good thing."

"I'm sorry I didn't get your call."

"Me too." He stared at her, unsure what to say next except that it was late and they both had things to do tomorrow. "I'll get you something to wear to sleep." He also grabbed what he needed from his room so he wouldn't have to go in and disturb her.

He left her gun on the nightstand and brought his into the living room. His couches were great for sleeping on—he'd fallen asleep many times watching a late movie or during a baseball game.

She stayed by the bedroom door.

Liam eased in, not moving fast, and kissed her cheek. "Sleep well."

"I'm sure I will."

He walked away from her because anything else was dangerous territory. He had to be the person he wanted to believe he was, one who did what he said he believed. Not because life was about following the rules he'd been taught to follow. But because he wanted to be a man of integrity. The kind of man he'd believed his father to be.

All of that had fallen apart. He wanted to prove it wasn't true, but if Vanguard pushed and it came out, then he'd have to acknowledge that his father had been a dirty cop. The alternative was that they found more to the story, and he had what he needed to bring the real conspiracy to light.

Becoming an officer like his dad had been about safeguarding the secret or finding out the truth. But that was years ago, and there were innocent lives to protect now. People like Karina and Roxie. To shield them, men like Raphi Obolensky needed to be behind bars.

And of course, the man targeting Roxie.

Whoever he was, Liam was going to find him.

TWENTY-ONE

Raphi Obolensky sat back in the booth against the red velvet seat. The table had been cleared of dirty dishes by one of the new servers. He'd watched her the entire time, pleased when she seemed aware of his attention.

Karina shifted beside him. He covered her knee with his hand, then squeezed her leg just above it so she knew he had not yet given her permission to move from his side.

She covered his hand with hers and stroked it, as though he wasn't digging his fingers in hard enough to leave bruises. She managed a wobbly smile. "I wasn't leaving. Just getting more comfortable here with you."

He let go because the feel of her hand on his made his skin crawl. He was tired of her and ready to move on, but the message had to be clear, nonetheless.

No one walked away from him.

He hadn't drawn the attention of the police by having his men drag her out of her house for his own amusement. Only so that no one else would ever think to try to go around him the way she had. Playing both sides. Keeping the police close, when he was the only authority here.

In Benson, Raphi Obolensky was king.

She ran two fingers over the bruise on her cheek she hadn't quite managed to hide with makeup. He liked her better with the blemish—since it gave a clear signal to anyone else with ideas.

After the disaster of his brother attempting to usurp his position, the climate right now meant he had to be swift and exacting with all punishment.

One of his men headed for the door. Raphi's awareness had the entire restaurant and everyone in it on his radar. After hours, they'd stayed, when the last customers exited, and had yet more drinks along with a few cigars so the smoke hung in the room, that rich tang of his father's study. The smell of it reminded him to be ruthless if he wanted to get ahead.

Kristo opened the door—likely alerted to someone outside by the man at the front. Both wore earpieces. The man who stepped in clutched a briefcase to his front. Cheeks flushed. Hair mussed. He was in his forties and wore an ill-fitting suit that hung awkwardly and a yellow tie.

"Doctor, come in." The man was a CEO and a renowned doctor of whatever-ology—Raphi didn't much care—and the go between for Raphi and the doctor's board of directors. "Have a seat."

"I don't want to take up too much of your time." Doctor Carlan shifted his weight from foot to foot in front of the table. "I just couldn't sit at home without bringing you the board's...concerns. We aren't sure—"

"There's no need to worry."

"The formula isn't finished! We can't make it work." Carlan flushed. "The board is unanimous in their belief that we should abandon the project if we can't find a solution to the problem. We simply don't have the money to—"

"Not only will you have the money," Raphi said. "You'll have the solution as well."

Carlan swallowed. "How is that poss—"

"Let me worry about that. It's why you brought me on board in the first place." Not that his father had given them much choice in the beginning. When his uncle took over after his father died, Raphi had kept the relationship going on the side, not giving his uncle a clue as to what he was doing.

These days, he didn't have to hide.

He also didn't have to claw so much for every inch of his position. All he had to do was keep a hold on it.

Behind the doctor, Kristo glanced at his associate, and they both grinned. Taking pleasure in the way Raphi continually cut off whatever the doctor wanted to say. A simple power play but effective.

Raphi shifted forward in his seat to lean into the table. "Now isn't the time for the board to become cowards. You need to stand up and lead them, Carlan. This is the way we arranged it. Unless you'd like us to find someone else to work with."

Carlan's mouth opened. He caught himself and said, "No. Of course not. I'll talk to them first thing in the morning."

"Good." Raphi nodded. "I have a man chasing the solution right now. As soon as it's solved, we'll have it for you." There was a lot riding on Morgan getting what they needed from the chemist, but everyone knew what would happen if they failed their part. "Not to worry."

"Yes, sir." Carlan nodded. "The board will be happy to hear that."

As if Raphi's answer was any different from what he'd

said the last time the doctor came in here saying the board was having second thoughts.

Raphi patted Karina's knee. "Go home with the doctor, dear. Keep him company tonight."

She uncrossed her knees, shifting to slide out of the booth away from him. A tiny note of escape crept into her body language.

He grabbed her and pulled her close enough to whisper in her ear. She let out a tiny mew of surprise and pain. He sucked in a breath through his nose, drawing in the odor of her fear. "Be convincing."

"Yes, Raphi."

He let her go. Watched her compose herself as she stood, then wind her arm with the doctor's and leave with him. Then he turned to his man. "Get word to Morgan. Tell him to light a fire under that chemist."

"Yes, sir." Kristo headed for the office.

Raphi lifted his glass and finished his whiskey. He needed that formula from the chemist if he was going to finish this. Otherwise, everything he'd been working on for years to build his empire would crumble to nothing, and he would be left with only rubble.

He wasn't going to let the police take it all away from him.

He and Liam O'Connell would have a reckoning.

And soon.

TWENTY-TWO

The second that Roxie walked into the office, Peter stood up from his desk. "I didn't think you'd be in today."

She shrugged. "Why not?"

He just stared at her. She dumped her bag and turned to sit on the edge of her desk so he could say what he wanted to. Which he did, sitting across from her the same way. "Because you were in a car accident last night?"

"It wasn't an accident, but I know what you mean." She pointed at herself. "Marine, plus seven hours of sleep, plus coffee, equals work."

Peter chuckled. "I figured it was something like that."

"So what have you got since we last touched base?"

"Quite a lot, actually." He turned to his computer, and she sat, then slid her chair across the floor to his desk. He glanced at her. "You walked a little stiff, but other than that, I wouldn't even know."

"It's not about pretending. It's about doing the job until I can finish the mission."

Peter hesitated.

"What?"

He lifted his coffee cup, realized it was empty, and set it back down.

"Spit it out."

He grinned. "Fine. Clare pulled Bob and I into a meeting at seven this morning."

It was just after nine now, and she had only just arrived for work. "About what?"

"She ran down the whole investigation into Mills' wife's disappearance and what you had figured out. Good work, by the way, following the trail here and putting together that this was where it all started."

She nodded. More coffee beckoned, but that was an avoidance tactic for facing reality. "He grew up in Seattle, but his family had a cabin over here. They spent a good chunk of summers in Benson, and Mark's father had business ties here."

"I've been looking into that. Have you, at all?"

"No." She shook her head. "What did you find?"

"A few bankrupt companies, failed startups. Even some investments into one of those multilevel marketing schemes that folded pretty spectacularly."

"I didn't get that deep. Did Mark have connections to any of it?" She'd never found a job he'd worked other than the Marines and figured he worked for cash as he said he'd done construction jobs around the northwest.

"Not on paper."

"What about the case we're supposed to be working?" She grinned. "The one the boss gave us?"

He chuckled. "Sure, sure." Peter clicked his mouse.

"Please tell me we get to go kick a door in today. I need to burn some energy." Her entire body ached from whiplash, but she'd told the truth about the amount of sleep she got.

Being in Liam's room had been odd at first, then familiar in its scents and style. She'd fallen quickly into a deep sleep that felt like twice as long as it was, and she'd woken up to hot coffee and pain meds. The man was a dream come true, but all that did was make her regret the way her life had gone.

She could argue she hadn't thought herself worthy of a man like Liam O'Connell. That it would've been too comfortably easy. She wouldn't have been able to handle it without doubting every second if she deserved to be on the receiving end of what he could give her.

The truth was, she'd made the absolute wrong choice and turned her life in a direction that nearly killed her. Like anyone in an abusive situation, it had been too late when she realized what had become of her life.

"Sadly, this may not end in door-kicking."

"Darn." Roxie went over and filled two mugs with coffee.

When she returned, Peter had pulled up a bunch of documents on her computer.

"Should I be worried you did that without my login?"

"Admin credentials." He grinned. "I took a look at the board of Hurstwhile and started to run each of the members—also all the other heads of departments. We're looking at every single person who works for them now or has worked for them over the past fifteen years."

"That's a lot of people."

"Divide and conquer." He pointed at her screen. "There are some interesting inconsistencies in a couple of their investment portfolios, though nothing that would have drawn the attention of the IRS." He clicked her mouse, and an online newspaper article popped up. "Six months ago, their head of research died suddenly."

"Car accident?"

He twisted his shoulders around to stare at her. "Car accident…"

"Was it?"

"No, but I'll circle back to that in a second. There's something else I found."

Roxie said, "Okay, tell me about the head of research."

"Tuesday morning, earlier this year. Suddenly, he just drops dead in his lab. Heart attack." He scrolled using her mouse. "They tried to save his life, but he didn't respond."

Roxie blew out a breath. "I have some field medical training and a Basic Life Support cert, but situations like that are scary for everyone."

"Since his death, all forward progress in research has ground to a halt. Treatment has continued as far as they've reported it to the governing body, but I called a couple of registered patients. I explained exactly who I am and that we're looking at the company, and they volunteered of their own volition the fact they haven't received treatment since the doctor's death."

"Really."

Peter nodded. "Those on experimental protocols have stopped being given appointments. Prescriptions are being refilled, but nothing new is being done."

"So they're in a holding pattern."

"Seems like it."

Roxie sipped her coffee. "They don't have anyone to come up with new stuff."

"Which means they should never have risked the facility like that, putting all their eggs in the basket of what one doctor can come up with."

She set her coffee down and stretched her arms above her head, dragging the hem of her sweater with her. If she pulled her sleeves up, Peter would see the wrap she'd asked Liam for that she'd put on her wrist. An old injury she'd had to explain how she got when Mark twisted her arm viciously one time. Liam had helped her secure the wrap since it was difficult to do on her own.

Then he'd kissed her forehead and told her she was beautiful.

The man was a conundrum she didn't know how to solve.

She lowered her arms back down and sighed. It would be tough to sit at a desk all day when she was already this antsy. She would need to get out and walk at lunch or go up to the gym and run. The latter option was safer, and she wouldn't waste the time of whatever protection detail Clare would put on her if she went outside.

Liam had driven her here personally this morning. If she had to have armed guards for weeks to come, it was going to get old. Unless it was Liam. But she could hardly take up that much of his time for an indeterminate period. That wasn't fair.

The man had a life and a career. She didn't necessarily fit into it.

"If the board is still operating like everything is fine," Peter said, "then sooner or later the problems will become more apparent than just what we've discovered."

"But how many patients have to suffer who should be receiving treatment before someone like the media, or the public, or the police notice?"

Peter nodded, a thoughtful expression on his face.

"Does it tie back to our homeless man's death and Liam's father's death?"

"I think we're going to need a homicide cop and a prosecutor to tell us the answer to that question." He sat back, impressing her. Not many young people took a humble approach—or anyone, really, these days.

"And if we do find a responsible party, it could be the dead doctor. Who else could be liable except the Hurstwhile Center as a whole?"

Peter nodded.

If only she could give Liam closure over his father's death, but she might not be able to do so. At least, not in a way that would satisfy a question he had never found an answer to enough to resolve for himself what had happened.

Peter's phone rang. He snapped it up. "Olson." A second passed, and then he said, "Yeah, boss." When he hung up, he turned to her. "Let's go. Bob's office."

Roxie followed him over and into the tiny closet Bob called an office. The older man had paled from his usual color. "What's up, boss?"

"The niece you spoke to?"

"Sierra Turner?" Roxie asked.

Bob nodded. "She was mugged on the way from their parking lot to the hospital this morning. She's in the ICU in critical condition. Someone bashed her head in."

Roxie winced. "Because we talked to her." Peter turned to look at her, so she said, "It's not a coincidence."

"No," Bob agreed. "It isn't a coincidence. It means we're getting close to something."

"And if people are going to get hurt," Roxie said, "then is it really worth it? Someone could get killed. Sierra could still die."

"So we should quit?"

Roxie shook her head. "That's not what I said. But we need to be smart and make a plan."

Peter's jaw flexed. "I need to show you something."

A cold pulse of dread spread through her gut. What now?

TWENTY-THREE

Officer Gutierrez knocked on the huge oak doors at the front of the Obolensky house. Liam spotted the camera doorbell, though both he and Gutierrez were at the edge of the view with where they were standing.

Not that they'd be blindsiding Raphi, showing up here just past breakfast—for the crowd who'd stayed out until three.

He had dropped Roxie off at work and done a couple of hours of briefings, meetings with his chief, and paperwork. Now he held himself back from calling to see how her day was going. There was a case to work, like always. When was there not a case to work? But being a professional, not a guy who just thought about a beautiful woman all day when he was supposed to be focused, was a better plan.

The door swung open.

The older woman who answered wore pants, a white blouse, an apron, and flat shoes. "Can I help you?" Her voice held the accent of the Obolensky mother country. "Officers?"

Likely that was a signal to anyone in the house who might be unaware there were cops at the door.

Gutierrez said, "We'd like to speak with Mr. Raphael Obolensky." He didn't ask if Raphi was in because they all knew he was. Liam had ordered a squad car outside the house all night, so the officers had seen Raphi come home alone in the car—except for his driver—just before three.

"Right this way." She stepped back and admitted them.

The inside of the house smelled like candles, cigars, and like someone had thrown up port on the rug at some point. This housekeeper had probably been trying to get rid of the smell since.

"Thank you, ma'am." Gutierrez turned on the professional charm. "We appreciate you allowing us in. We won't be more than a few minutes."

"Please follow me."

That likely meant Raphi knew they were here even before they knocked on the front door. Liam scanned the hall as they followed the housekeeper to an open door at the end. They passed a cracked door with a couple of people inside muttering in conversation. Liam heard, "While," but nothing else, so that was nothing regarding surveillance.

Not that anything they overheard would be what they needed for a warrant. It would never be probable cause for a search. Not unless they had reason to believe Karina was being held here against her will.

The housekeeper stopped at the door. "Mr. Obolensky, the police are here."

"*Spasibo*, Maria. That will be all." He waved her away, a king on his throne behind the desk.

Maria shut the doors, closing them in the study. All wood and old books. A fireplace, empty right now except for ash. A state-of-the-art computer completely at odds with the old-world feel of the room and its velvet high-backed chairs.

"Sergeant O'Connell." Raphi took a drag on a cigar.

They stopped about six feet in front of the desk. No one wanted to get within arm's reach of a guy like this, even if he had no visible weapons.

"Raphi," Liam said. "How's business?" He didn't wait for an answer, just motioned to the cop beside him. "This is Gutierrez. He has questions."

"Training the next generation in the art of annoying honest citizens."

"Yes." Liam nodded, stone-faced. "It's an art form we work years to perfect."

Gutierrez snorted under his breath. "Sir, we're investigating a missing woman, and we are aware the two of you are connected." He pulled out his phone and, for a second, looked like he wanted to ask His Honor if he had permission to approach the bench. Gutierrez stepped forward and showed Raphi the screen. "Karina went missing yesterday. We're looking for her, asking everyone who knows her if they've seen her."

Raphi couldn't argue that he didn't know her since they'd explained they knew of a connection. They had proof of it on the burner phone they'd found under Karina's bed.

A phone that wasn't hers.

It had pictures of them together, but not selfies. Maybe they weren't aware they were being photographed, which begged the question of where Karina got the phone. Or had someone dropped it when they took her from her house?

Also on the phone were texts depicting drug deals—emojis that the police knew were used by dealers and customers. They'd been able to decipher most of it.

Then there were calls to Karina's phone, and Raphi's, and

a list of others they were looking up. A treasure trove of information they would be unpacking for at least a few days. But enough to get them here to ask Raphi if he'd seen her—and get a look at the inside of his house.

"This is about your brother, Liam? You think I retaliated by kidnapping your friend?"

Liam wasn't going to take the bait. "You've left Conrad alone. I've got no beef with you." Not since he'd stopped leaning on Liam's brother for protection money. Just so Backdraft Pizza and Grill could continue to operate.

The second that Liam had heard about what was happening—how two guys from Obolensky's crew had roughed up Conrad and given him a black eye—he'd stepped in and put a stop to it.

Put himself on Raphi's radar.

That old-world mafia strong-arming people didn't work now. Especially not in Benson. Liam had made sure the message was clearly communicated through Raphi's men, straight to him. So what if the guy was trying to carve out his own territory and build a reputation in town for himself. He wasn't going to use Liam's family to do it.

"Just tell us where she is." Liam shrugged one shoulder. "Then we'll be on our way."

Raphi glanced to the side where Liam spotted a door cracked open. He couldn't see through it even an inch. Just the angled door. Raphi turned back to them and took another drag on his cigar.

"Those will kill you, you know?" Liam couldn't resist saying it.

Raphi grinned. "Nice of you to care about me."

He stared at the guy, all slick shirt and shined shoes. Like a used car salesman, except he sold death and dealt in fear as currency. More than likely he'd set the bomb that killed his uncle, Matvei Obolensky, over the summer. Or it had been his brother Nico. Whichever brother had ordered the underling to set the bomb didn't matter. Raphi's kingdom wasn't going to last long.

The side door swung open.

"Karina." He started to walk toward her but held himself back.

She headed right for Raphi, wearing a pair of white pants and a blouse that draped off one shoulder. Full makeup—thick enough to cover nearly anything—and her hair perfectly styled. But when she smiled, he knew it wasn't real.

"Liam." She stood beside Raphi and put her hand on his shoulder.

"I haven't heard from you since you called me," Liam said. "Everything all right?"

"Why wouldn't it be?"

Gutierrez took over. "Ma'am, you reported intruders in your house. I'd like to take your statement, per that matter. Preferably in private."

Raphi said nothing.

Karina shook her head. "That won't be necessary. I wanna withdraw my report—or however that works. Liam probably misunderstood what I said."

"Kar—"

She cut him off, something Raphi seemed to think extremely funny. "Liam, I've told you more than once that I'm not interested in you like that. Maybe you had an...arrangement with my sister, but that's not going to happen with me. You need to leave me alone, or I'll be forced to report you for harassment."

Gutierrez looked at him.

Liam clenched down on his back teeth and said nothing.

"I'm glad you're safe, ma'am," Gutierrez said. "If you need

any assistance, don't hesitate to call 911. The police are here to help you stay safe."

"Thank you." She gave an unconvincing smile and left the way she'd come in.

Liam watched her for signs of injury but saw nothing.

"Let's go, Sarge." Gutierrez led the way.

Liam didn't look back. He wasn't interested in the smirk that would no doubt be on Raphi's face right now. *You win this time.* Except all he wanted was to ensure Karina was safe. She'd sounded scared. Now she flipped it back and made it sound like he'd been harassing her?

What was with this woman?

It made no sense to him.

Either she had what she wanted, or they were working together to protect something already in motion that couldn't be stopped.

Which was it, and how deeply was Karina involved?

TWENTY-FOUR

P eter drove, so when Roxie's phone rang, she answered and held it to her ear.

She had been waiting for Destiny to call her back. "Hey, girl. How was your night?"

"That's it?" Destiny huffed. "How was my night?"

"I'd feel the same way if I spent all evening with Jasper and he stayed over." Just a little dig and a smile. Peter glanced over, but Roxie would have to explain later that they had a running thing about Destiny and her crush on Jasper that she liked to deny.

"We're not talking about me!"

Roxie chuckled. "I'm good."

Peter turned the corner faster than reasonable, so she grabbed the door handle with her free hand and made a face like she was scared for her life. He grinned. "Don't be a baby."

"Good? You spent the night at Liam's," Destiny wailed. "Did you... Tell me you didn't! I thought he was a good guy!"

"Destiny, chill." Roxie glanced at the window. "He slept on the couch."

Peter said, "Good."

Destiny, through the phone, echoed the same word.

"I thought you said faith wasn't about doing the right things." Why was it such a big deal that they'd adhered to a standard most people in the world couldn't give two hoots about? Liam was a good guy. What did Destiny expect? Roxie had been out of it, in shock and traumatized. Not to mention the whiplash. Hardly the time to get...romantic.

As if romance had ever ended well for her.

If she did have a relationship again—big *if*—she would do it the right way. Proper. After all, it couldn't possibly hurt to wait, and the outcome might even be better for once in her life.

"Faith isn't about doing the right thing like you have to measure up," Destiny said.

Roxie gripped the phone and listened as if her life depended on it—which it might.

"It's about doing it because you want to. Not out of obligation."

"Huh." Roxie figured, on face value, there wasn't much difference. Then again, maybe it was about intention instead of the outward action. She needed to learn more if she was going to get into it. Everyone around her seemed to be a Christian. It wasn't something she could avoid anymore. Not when Liam's Bible had been on his nightstand.

She'd opened it and found his father's name inside the front cover, and then she'd leafed through and looked at where he'd made notes in the margin. Until it felt too much like intruding, and she'd set it down.

Peter pulled onto a residential street, their destination.

She said, "I've gotta get back to work, but I'll call you later."

"Sure, sure." Destiny used, like brushing Roxie off when she didn't want to.

"What's going on?"

"I'm good."

"Are you?" Roxie had enough people forcing her to be honest that she could repay the favor with Destiny. Get her to spill her worries and trust Roxie to carry that burden. "What's going on?"

"I'll tell you later. It'll keep."

"As long as it will." Maybe it was about Jasper.

"I just decided something, that's all. I'll tell you about it at dinner."

"Or lunch. We might come by Backdraft to eat." She glanced at Peter, who nodded. "I'll text you."

"Thanks, Rox."

They parked and headed together to the front door. Both of them had ID cards that proved they worked for Vanguard, which carried some weight with the local community.

Roxie knocked on the front door of a tiny gray house with a red door and flowerpots beside the stoop. The flower beds needed weeding, and the plants might be those ones that came back every year, so you didn't have to keep planting more.

She'd wanted land and a garden once. Maybe planters of vegetables. Even a dog.

Not things that worked in a townhome with no garden.

Roxie had so much "one day" and "probably wouldn't happen" bottled up inside her that it was a wonder she didn't explode.

The door cracked open. An older woman with a walker stood there, staring at them through bottle-thick glasses. A halo of white curls encircled her head. She wore a polyester pair of pants and a knit sweater.

"Good morning, ma'am." Roxie took the lead in

explaining who they were. "We understand your son lives here with you, is that correct? We'd like to speak with him."

She frowned. "Elyan hasn't lived here in years. He doesn't come around anymore, but he left all his stuff."

Which was exactly why they were here.

Another person had been killed in a car accident where the body burned up on impact. Not exactly what happened in her case, but close enough. So far, it connected to the nurse who'd died years ago before she could speak to Sierra.

Too many similar incidents to be a coincidence, even if she was inclined to believe that. Which she wasn't.

"Would it be okay if we came in? It's pretty chilly out here, and I wouldn't want to raise your heating bill."

"Yes, dear." She shuffled back, and they stepped into the foyer. "Would you like some tea, dear?"

"I could make it," Peter offered. "My mother taught me how. I still drink tea when I need to sit and find some clarity. Remember her a little bit."

The older woman completely melted, faced with a handsome young man who loved his mother and drank tea. "Let's go into the kitchen. I think I have some biscuits."

She had a slight trace of an Eastern European accent.

As Roxie moved behind them, she said, "Is it okay if I use your restroom, ma'am?"

"Oh, call me Ethel."

"Thank you, Ethel. I'm Roxanne."

The older lady said, "Second door down the hall, on the left."

"Thanks." Roxie headed for it and peeked in, then closed the door while still in the hallway. She kept going, easing doors open until she found the room she was looking for. Not the old lady's bedroom, nor a storage room that had once been a place to sew.

The room she stepped into had a twin bed that had been stripped to its mattress, an aging desk tucked against the opposite wall, and a dresser covered with items that blocked the mirror, some old seventies piece of furniture that would outlive any of the new stuff.

She checked under the bed and found it clear. The desk had an ancient computer, not as much longevity as the dresser. It would probably be obsolete—the kind of thing that would make Peter wince and mutter. The kid had been spoiled by Vanguard tech.

She couldn't carry the tower out, so she stuck in the flash drive Peter had given her. She didn't have to touch anything or boot anything up according to his instructions. She only had to make sure the light on top flashed green. That it kept going.

When it turned red, she could remove it and be on her way.

Until then...

She leafed through desk drawers that seemed to be a catchall spot for pens, scissors, rulers, sticky notes, and several batteries in odd sizes with no matching pair. Who needed three C batteries without needing a fourth?

She found nothing taped under the drawers.

Dresser next. Roxie didn't shift things around too much in case someone checked after she'd been in here. She found an envelope taped under the lowest drawer and tucked it into her pocket since it was only letter size.

The flash drive switched over to solid green, then turned red. Whatever that meant, it wasn't flashing anymore, so she pulled it out and pocketed it.

She slipped back out into the hall, went in the bathroom, and flushed in case Ethel was listening for the sound of her being done. She washed her hands because who knew what germs had been on Elyan's things.

Then she headed back to the kitchen for tea, smiling as she entered. "Thank you. I really needed to go."

Ethel had Peter fill the teapot. "Set it on the table, dear." She waved him over from her seat, then said, "You sit as well, dear. We'll have a chat."

Roxie pulled out the chair.

The doorbell rang.

"My goodness. Two visits in one day. In the same hour!"

Roxie smiled. "Would you like me to see who it is?"

"Thank you, dear."

Peter came with her. Roxie unclipped the fastener on her gun but didn't draw it. She kept her hand near it and opened the door.

Two uniformed patrol cops, both older, stood on the doorstep.

"Ma'am," the one to the left said, "we've had reports of a disturbance at this residence. Please exit the house."

The other said, "You, too, sir."

"Is the resident home?" The cop reached for her arm, and Roxie pulled back. Just a protective reflex. He frowned. "Step out of the house, ma'am. Now. Keep your hands where I can see them."

TWENTY-FIVE

Liam stepped out of the conference room, careful not to breathe a visible sigh of relief. He checked the time on his watch—time for more coffee—and headed for the break room on this floor. He'd been called in to explain what happened at Raphi's.

Gutierrez had filed his report, including Karina's statement. The fact it matched Liam's statement about their visit to Obolensky played in their favor. Telling the truth always should.

He'd given the whole rundown of the relationship he'd had with Karina over the years and all the particulars of the time they'd spent together. All of it had been in public, so he had nothing to worry about. But accusations, even casual ones, always had to be followed up on for everyone's integrity.

Not to mention that the department didn't need any more scandals.

He stepped into the empty break room and relaxed a bit. The pot was full, and he borrowed a mug with the department logo on it and filled it as far as it would go. He took a couple of seconds to sip and let his mind think of nothing at all, just so he could get a break. The same peace and quiet he felt while running.

He should ask Roxie if she wanted to go for a run. After she no longer had whiplash from the truck crash.

Now that he knew Karina was fine, or as fine as she wanted to be, he could focus back on Roxie and what was happening with her. The fact she'd been in an abusive relationship with someone he'd known and allowed to watch his back, a guy he'd relied on, stuck in him like a piece of sour candy lodged in his throat.

It was a good thing the guy was dead, or he and Liam would be having words.

Which begged the question of *who* was appearing in her life pretending to be Mark and terrorizing her. Causing that accident. Sending her that snake. Destiny's house had full surveillance now, but Roxie wasn't going to stay there in lock-down. He respected her need to feel free too much to ask her to do that.

He should chat with Gage, see what Clare had to say and find out if there was a plan in the works from Vanguard to get this guy.

Put a stop to the terrorizing.

Roxie needed the chance to heal and move on with her life.

"Hey, *Sarge*." An older patrol officer strode in, followed by another. Both had gray temples. Rounder middles. The kind of guys who accepted all those free lunches the public liked to give to on-duty cops. Liam let Conrad give him the family discount at Backdraft, but he still paid his way. These guys were old school.

Like Liam's father.

He lifted his chin. "How is it out there?"

The second officer said, "Had an interesting callout."

The first guy poured two coffees, and they both leaned against the counter to shoot the breeze. No one sat at the round table covered with trashy magazines, or the couch that looked like it had been there since the seventies. If anyone tried to move it, the thing would probably spontaneously combust.

"Oh yeah?" Liam needed to get going, but cops liked to tell stories.

"Yeah," the first cop said. "You should keep a tighter leash on your girl, Sarge."

Liam frowned. "What's that?"

"Rox-*anne*." The cop smirked. "Sticking her nose into things, places it doesn't belong. Hassling a sweet old woman and causing trouble."

The other guy nodded, one elbow on the counter, the other hand holding his mug. "Her and that partner." He raised his brows, as though something untoward was going on that Liam needed to get a clue about.

"So, she was just doing her job for Vanguard?" He wasn't going to argue their definition of harassment. He could read the report himself and then talk to Roxie.

Both of them snorted.

"That company." One shook his head. "They're all the same. No offense to Lieutenant DeLuca." The guy pushed off the counter and faced off with Liam.

His gut tightened. "They have their jobs; we have ours."

"Yeah," the cop said, his tone hard. "And ours is to keep them from harassing people and digging up stuff that needs to be left to lie, right, Sarge? Things that should stay dead."

Like his father? Liam's jaw hardened.

"You of all people should know that the past needs to stay where it is. Doesn't help anyone if it's all dragged up again, right?" The officer lifted his coffee cup. "The department doesn't need another black mark."

Liam turned to face the guy straight on, about to speak when Blake and Jasper strode in.

"Hey, Sarge, got a minute?" Blake led the way, an assessing expression in his eyes as his gaze switched between Liam and the two older cops.

They'd read the room and knew exactly what was happening. Liam stepped back and took a sip of his coffee. Then he nodded. "Sure. We can head down to the cave, get back to work."

"Good deal," Jasper said. "The coffee up here sucks."

"That's because you're a snob." Blake shoved Jasper's shoulder.

Liam dumped the rest of his drink in the sink and upended the cup. "Let's go." He reached the door, then glanced back at the cops. "Have a good one." He lifted his chin, then left.

No one said anything all the way downstairs, not with an officer in the elevator with them, until the guy broke off and headed for the parking lot end of the basement. The cave was where SWAT had their offices. Soon to be renovated for whatever they were doing with the offices and equipment down here. Repurposing things, and people.

"Those guys were harassing you, right?" Jasper eyed him.

Liam headed through the main room where they discussed plans and put cases together. He stopped at their table, the surface of it was a computer itself that connected to the monitors on the walls. "It's no big deal. I just need to make sure they didn't push Peter and Roxie around."

"Because you need to protect them from the cops?" Blake folded his arms, his thinking pose.

Liam just leaned back against the table. He glanced at Jasper. "I thought you said there would be more coffee?"

"Just talk." Jasper lifted his chin. "You let them hassle you?"

"It's no big deal. They said what they had to say, and now it's done."

"It's not okay. You should talk to their sergeant. Get them written up for being belligerent."

Technically, Liam did outrank them, but it was a delicate balance when an officer had years—or decades—more experience than their superior, who was younger and brought a whole lot of innovative ideas. "I'll see if it's a pattern, but it's more likely a one-off."

Blake said, "That just means it's personal."

"Which means they're being unprofessional." Jasper wasn't going to let this go.

Liam pressed his lips together.

"What did they say?" Blake wasn't going to back down either.

"They reminded me that my father's service record doesn't need something coming to light that puts a stain on his memory or the department."

"So they're trying to bully you into not finding the truth."

Liam glanced at Jasper. "It's not that simple."

"So explain it," Blake said.

Liam sighed. "They were at my father's funeral. I needed air, so I headed outside. Ran into them in the middle of a conversation. It was pretty clear they needed whatever my dad was into to stay quiet."

"So they insinuated he was dirty?" Jasper's expression made it plain he didn't agree with that. "That's crazy. My dad knew your dad. Said he was the most solid guy he'd ever met."

"Really?" Liam's brows rose. "You've never told me that."

Jasper shrugged his shoulder. "Cops usually don't give weight to the opinion of a guy in politics."

"Maybe they should." If the politician was as solid as the cop.

Blake said, "Don't let them push you around. They're probably only trying to cover their own butts."

Liam nodded.

Jasper said, "Now, tell us what this is about, SWAT being shifted from full-time to a collateral duty team where we're just on call."

Liam swallowed and nearly choked on it. "You know?"

"Just found out," Blake said. "And you didn't tell us. What's up with that?"

They'd had his back with those other cops. Told him not to be pushed around. And they *knew* he'd withheld information about their careers? Warmth infused every part of him. His brothers in this room wouldn't abandon him. They'd stick it out, even when things changed, and he didn't have to feel like he was losing them.

Maybe he never would.

Jasper said, "I filled out the paperwork to take the detective exam."

"I'm taking the sergeant exam." Blake wiggled his brows.

Liam started to laugh.

Blake stepped over. "I'm comin' for you, bro."

Liam swung his arm around Blake's neck, both of them laughing.

TWENTY-SIX

Roxie slid into the corner booth at Backdraft, just because she needed to see Destiny and find out what her friend wanted to tell her before she headed to the house for the night. She didn't want to wait until Destiny had closed up at nearly midnight, cleaned up, and made it home—with an escort.

Who knew which officer was planning on babysitting her, and whether she could convince them she didn't need protection.

Peter waved for her to scoot over. Roxie went all the way around so she could get out the other side and not be boxed in. His brother, Simon, slid in beside him.

Peter said, "Selena will be here soon," with a smile he only reserved for the woman he'd started seeing over the summer.

Simon's smile wasn't quite as pleased. Not because he didn't like Selena, but probably more because his most recent relationship had turned out to be a disaster. Roxie still had him beat on that front, though.

"You guys were telling me about your run-in with the cops

this morning." Simon thanked the server for filling his water glass.

Roxie did the same, then added, "Can you tell Destiny we're here?"

The guy smiled. "Sure can."

"It wasn't so new for me. A run-in with cops." Peter smirked. "I'm just glad it wasn't one of the guys who arrested us."

Simon shared a grin with his twin.

Roxie said, "Until they ran your name and probably got your whole history." And hers.

Thankfully, most of what she'd gone through wasn't local and wasn't available to anyone outside of the military. Mark hadn't been retired like she was when they'd gotten together.

"Good thing it was on the up-and-up." Peter tapped the outside of her arm with the back of his hand.

Roxie explained to Simon, "The homeowner, whose son we are looking for, came out and told those meddling cops to leave us alone. That we were just there for tea. They didn't have a leg to stand on then, or when she threatened to call their supervisor and report them."

Simon grinned. Then he said, "I'm looking at the flash drive."

Roxie had been too freaked out to find it funny at the time, but now that it was over and done with, she could relax a bit. Let go of some of the tension she'd been carrying around all day, along with the ache of bruising from the whiplash. She'd taken off the wrist bandage earlier.

Right now, she needed food, or she was going to get hangry.

The door opened. Bob came in first, then stepped aside for an older woman.

A young guy behind the bar called out, "Mama's here!"

with a wide grin on his face. She waved at him, her smart watch slipping down her wrist. She wore pressed slacks and a blouse covered by a green military-style jacket. Straight blonde hair and newer canvas sneakers. She looked like a clothing catalog model.

Bob motioned in their direction, and she headed over.

Roxie got a look at her eyes and sucked in a breath. That ring of silver. "Liam's mother." She'd seen this woman in the Vanguard office but hadn't put it together. Now the similarity was so clear, and it was confirmed when Conrad stepped out of the kitchen, and they smiled at each other.

She hugged her son, then followed Bob to their booth. Bob shoved Simon over. The woman said, "Boys."

"Mrs. O'Connell." Peter waved. "How are you?"

"Fine, son. Simon?"

He nodded. "Nice to see you."

"And who is this?" She turned the full force of those silver eyes to Roxie. "I'm Olivia O'Connell."

"Roxanne." She scooted in, then held out her hand so they could shake. "Nice to meet you, Mrs. O'Connell."

She said, "Olivia is fine, as I've told these boys."

Bob grinned at her. "I'm not discouraging respect."

"Me either," Roxie said. "Kids these days seem like they need extra."

Peter gaped, then he shoved playfully at her shoulder.

She grinned. The front doors of the restaurant opened, and Liam strode in, followed by Blake and Jasper, who headed for the same high top table they'd been at before. Their table?

Liam spotted her.

She smiled, lifting two fingers as he headed for her like he didn't notice anyone else in the room.

Then he blinked. "Mom?"

"Right." Olivia tore the paper off her straw. "I guess it was inevitable."

Liam stood at the end of the table. "You're here."

"So I am."

"To talk about the case you're having Vanguard investigate?" Liam stared down at her, all that intensity present, but he seemed to hold himself back.

"What I do with my time and my money is my business, son."

His mouth shifted.

"But I'm sure Bob would be happy to fill you in with the progress they've made today."

Liam glanced around. "The old woman? I thought a couple of cops stopped you guys from talking to her."

Roxie said, "They tried, but she shut them down pretty quick. She doesn't know where her son is, though." She dug out her phone and found a picture of the guy they'd been trying to talk to. The financial manager that did the books for the Hurstwhile Center. "This guy."

Liam frowned. "For the veteran's death? This guy is an accountant for the Obolensky family. A Russian mafia family."

"Do you know where he is?" It was worth her asking.

Liam said, "I could probably find someone who knows where he is. But I'm also supposed to stay clear of the Russians for a while. Without a warrant."

Olivia smiled. "My son. Kicking butt and taking names."

Simon and Peter burst out laughing in tandem.

Roxie grinned.

Liam stared at her, an odd look on his face. "Have dinner with me over there." He pointed to a table in the corner, secluded from everyone else. "We can compare notes."

"This is a company dinner."

Bob said, "It isn't now." He waved for Olivia to move. "Get gone, girlie."

"I need to talk to Destiny, and we're supposed to go over the case." Roxie yelped. Liam's mom had her arm and started to drag her out of the booth.

"Go have dinner with my son. Please. The first live specimen in...what? Years?" She shot him a look of despair. "Don't screw this up. She seems nice, and I'll have more good-looking grandchildren." She glanced at the twins. "It makes for better Christmas cards. You can rub it in your friends' faces."

Liam stared at her. Simon and Peter laughed aloud.

Even Bob seemed like he was having trouble holding in his amusement.

Roxie's cheeks flamed. Everyone knew now. Not that she'd been trying to keep it a secret that she liked Liam. She wanted them to be close. As *friends*. This seemed more as though everyone thought they should be a couple. What could she say to dispel that notion?

Probably nothing.

Liam motioned with his head. "Let's go." Then he took off first, making a beeline to the table.

She wasn't sure if she should comply with that order, but the fact he'd done it that way and not in a way that felt like being subverted almost made it better. He wasn't going to pull punches. He would say it plain.

No games.

That was the only reason Roxie followed him. If the table of her friends and Liam's mom thought they were a thing, then what did everyone else think? She was a trainwreck on most days. Not the kind of woman Liam should saddle himself with.

He sat. She stood beside the table and stared at him. "We were next to each other outside Karina's house." She didn't want to say *together*, so instead said, "You let me drive your truck."

"Okay." He dragged the word out.

"What if Mark—or whoever it is—saw us."

He winced. "You think that's why he ran you off the road?"

"Maybe." She sank into the chair.

Behind her, a stool scraped across the floor, loud enough that she twisted around. Her whiplash aches flared to life, but she managed not to hiss too loud. Blake was on his way to the door, walking fast.

Jasper and Destiny stared after him. He said something to Destiny. She shook her head and wound her way over to Roxie.

She stood and hugged her friend because it seemed like Destiny needed that. "What's going on?" Did it have to do with what Destiny had said she wanted to tell Roxie?

The other woman sighed. "I told him what I decided."

Liam said, "And what's that?"

"I'm leaving in the new year." Destiny lifted her chin. "For a six-month mission trip overseas."

TWENTY-SEVEN

L iam's brows rose.

"I know." Destiny sighed. "I know. But should he really be surprised?"

"Could just be wishful thinking that he wasn't going to have to worry about if you were safe, outside his sphere."

Roxie glanced over and nodded.

Destiny sighed. "So I should never venture outside the area where he can be one of the first to respond? He knows I want to travel. That I want to help people."

Roxie tugged her friend to her side. "He'll come around. He's just scared for you."

Destiny made a face. "I have to get back to work. You guys want the specials, right?" She hurried off before either of them could say otherwise.

Roxie sat across from him and laid her napkin on her lap. He glanced around. They were in the date corner. *Great.* Everyone was going to think something of it when all he'd done was point at the closest empty table.

She glanced at the window beside them.

"Everything okay?" He studied her. In the past twenty-four hours, she'd been in an accident and harassed by the police.

"Did you have to call insurance about your truck?"

He nodded. "They're compiling the paperwork. I'm going to borrow Gage's car until the weekend when I can go get a new truck."

She sighed.

"I'm just glad you're not hurt." He wanted to reach out and cover her hand with his but was pretty sure that was his mom peering around the back of the bench seat to look them. "That's what counts."

"Thank you." Her gaze drifted to the window again, and she sucked in a breath.

"What is it?"

She paled. "I thought I saw him." Her gaze scanned outside, through the window. Liam turned and looked as well. Beyond the parking lot were the storefronts in this strip mall: an outdoors store, footwear, and chain clothing at awesome prices.

"Where did you see him?" Liam shifted in his seat.

"It was probably nothing." She gave him a sardonic smile. "He's dead, remember?"

"I've been thinking about that. Maybe it's someone who just looks a whole lot like him." Liam sat back so Destiny could put a pasta dish in front of him. She set a loaded cheese-burger in front of Roxie and then disappeared again.

They grinned at each other and then switched plates.

Liam grabbed the burger. "Thanks."

Roxie took a bite.

Before he dug in, he said, "I think it's probably a cousin, or maybe he has a brother? Did he ever mention any family to you?"

She shook her head.

"How long were you together?"

"Too long."

Okay. "Were you married?"

"No, thankfully." She flinched. "Not grade A on the morals, I'm afraid, but I'm glad I dragged my feet on that. He was pushing. I think it was the catalyst for me wanting to get out. Before I ended up any deeper." She shifted on her chair. "He got orders saying that he was being deployed for nine months. He never would've left me at home. I think that played into him trying to kill both of us."

She glanced at the window again.

Liam ran a thumb over the back of her hand. "Maybe it's calloused to say this, but you're alive, and he's not. I'm not going to lose sleep over it."

She nodded but didn't look at him. She turned her hand and held on for a second. "I wonder how I could've been so stupid. Why I didn't realize what was happening before it was too late? How I could've fallen for it without seeing below the surface."

Liam might've done the same with Karina, considering she'd strung him along by claiming to have nothing to do with the Russians, and now she was practically in bed with them. He wanted to sit her down and ask how long that had been going on and why she was with them when she'd been so angry over her sister's involvement. Maybe that was because Veronika had been a confidential informant, giving him information on them rather than Karina's more sympathetic route.

After dinner he drove her to Destiny's. A few minutes later, a uniformed officer he'd known for a long time pulled up to sit on the house for the night. Liam shot the breeze with him while Roxie went inside. It was time to call it a night, but tomorrow, he'd go back to the office to run some names, to find out if Mark had siblings or cousins he shared a resemblance with.

First thing the next morning, after he forced himself to work out at the gym because he needed it, he sat at his desk and pulled up the database so he could search some more. His mom had messaged him during his workout to tell him that she loved Roxie. With heart emojis. Not something that needed a reply when he'd rather talk to her about the Vanguard case.

He called her, but she didn't pick up. But this morning might be the day she had that ladies' Bible study.

Half an hour later, he had a list of names. He'd check their social media accounts first since it usually proved a treasure trove of information—and photos—and it was all public. The desk phone rang, and he put it to his ear. "Sergeant O'Connell."

"This is Ethan, down at county lockup. We just opened for visiting, and one of the names you gave us? He just signed in."

Liam didn't recognize the voice, and he knew most of the officers down at the jail. This one must be new. "Which name?"

"Raphael Obolin...Oblong..."

"Obolensky."

"Maybe," Ethan said. "I'm not great with names. Anyway, he checked in, and he's meeting with one of our inmates."

"Morgan Alakov?"

"Nah...someone else. I'll have to go look up the name."

"I'm on my way. Make sure you get it all recorded, all right?"

"Copy that." Ethan hung up.

Liam grabbed his things and stood. Blake and Jasper were both at their desks, running information on the accountant that Vanguard was looking into. They were trying to nail down the connection between him and the Hurstwhile Center—to see if there was a correlation between that place and the Russian family they were trying to take down.

"I'm headed to the jail. Raphi's there."

Jasper asked, "Morgan?"

He shook his head.

"Probably the guy he was talking to in the cafeteria."

Liam agreed. "Maybe he's there to pick up whatever they asked him for." Which Liam would be able to find out since all those conversations were observed. Anything that passed between them could be intercepted.

He slung his backpack over his shoulder and headed for his car.

The drive would take him past the Vanguard building, just off the freeway on the edge of the Benson city limits. He didn't want to think about Roxie, but that was pretty inevitable at this point.

Five minutes into the twelve-minute drive, he was doing sixty-seven in the fast lane when a Hummer came up behind him. The vehicle sped up and tapped the back of Gage's car.

Liam gripped the wheel. This was what had happened to Roxie, and it had been the Mark look-alike who'd nearly killed her. He selected on the dash screen to call emergency dispatch, giving his name and badge number. "I need backup now, or there's going to be a multi-car pileup on the freeway."

"I'm sorry, sir, we don't have that badge number on file."

"Yeah, you do." It was the same number his dad had worn. When Liam graduated from the police academy, the chief at the time had asked if he wanted his father's badge, and Liam had told him yes without hesitating.

"That number was retired several years ago when the officer in question was killed." The dispatcher continued,

"Please do not tie up the 911 service with prank calls, sir. Or you will be reported to the police. This is your one and only warning."

"But—"

The dispatcher hung up.

Liam gaped at the screen. Behind him, the Hummer slammed into the back of the car again. Liam gripped the wheel. A car pulled alongside him, and he glanced over in time to see the rear driver's side window lowering. An AR-15 leaned out the window.

Uh-oh. Liam squeezed the wheel and swung it right, directly into the side of their car. It sped to the right and slammed into another car.

Both spun out. The Hummer engine roared behind him.

Liam spotted the exit for Vanguard and pointed his car toward it, flipping on lights and sirens in case it gave someone an extra second to get out of his way.

He barreled down the exit lane with the Hummer right behind him.

Bullets peppered the back window from someone leaning out the passenger side window. Glass shattered. Rounds pinged off the side and back of the car.

Liam ducked his head.

He turned the corner at the bottom of the off-ramp and, at the last second, had to swerve around a Prius.

The Hummer clipped its back end and sent the electric car spinning out of control.

Liam turned hard and fast into the Vanguard parking lot, tipping the car up onto two wheels in the process.

Bullets sprayed the car.

He hit the gas and drove toward the only help he might get while dialing the Vanguard front desk. When the receptionist picked up, he yelled, "Incoming!"

TWENTY-EIGHT

Roxie patted down the tab on the vest as fast as she could, her hair already back in a ponytail. "Go."

Peter went first out the side door. Both of them had pistols. Bob had an old rifle, though she'd have to ask him if he was allowed to have a registered firearm with his criminal history. The rest of Vanguard—or so it seemed—poured out of the other doors. She could picture them in her mind, running out like ants as they ran down the left side of the building to the front corner.

Peter peered around.

Gunshots filled the air out front.

"I don't see Liam." Peter pulled back. "But if he's in that car, he's pinned down."

"Let's go."

The person behind them said, "I'll cover you."

Bullets slammed into the side of the car that Liam had driven her home in last night. She was the one who was supposed to be in danger, not him.

Peter ran for the cover of the car, and she raced after him, keeping her eyes open. She spotted movement in the

Hummer and fired at the window. Someone poked their head up on the far side, gun in hand. Her round hit the metal under the bottom ledge of the window.

They ducked behind the car. A round hit the roof right in front of where she'd been standing.

She let out a breath. "At least four, with the two in there." One guy was firing at the car and the Vanguard building from over the hood, another from over the roof near the driver's side door.

"Copy that." Peter held the buttons on the side of his phone like a walkie-talkie and relayed that. Simon's voice responded.

Roxie eased past him and pulled the door handle up. From her crouched position, she had to reach up to it, then scoot out of the way so she could get the door open. Liam lay slumped on the seat. She spotted blood on his side, just below his ribs. Had the bullet gone into his stomach?

Roxie gasped. "Liam?!"

She turned to Peter. "Cover me. He's hit!"

She heard him relaying that information as the world around her blurred into sights and sensations. No idea what she did with her gun, but she got both hands under his arms, grabbed hard, and slid his upper body onto the passenger seat.

Roxie gritted her teeth. She needed to stand up so she could get him all the way out and get under him. She'd have to carry him.

Roxie shifted back on her behind and pulled him out of the car on top of her. He stirred. "I've got you." To Peter, she said, "Check that his feet aren't twisted or caught."

He reached in. "Clear."

Roxie backed up in a scoot and pulled him with her. Liam lay on top of her. "We need cover. And he needs a medic." She twisted and looked at the building. "Medic!"

"Inside." Peter glanced to the side. "Cops."

She heard the sirens then. Someone who was set up at a window inside squeezed off a shot with a sniper rifle. Then another person. Inside the Hummer, whoever they were screamed. The police sirens grew louder.

The Hummer door slammed, the engine revved, and they pulled out.

Making a run from a greater force?

She said, "Are we clear?"

Peter looked for a second. "Clear."

She rolled, got her head under Liam's arms, and stood with his weight on her. Teeth gritted. More than one person ran toward them to help her.

"Inside." That sounded like Clare, or maybe the woman Roxie had met at their morning meeting. Some federal agent and her husband, who was also a federal agent.

The doors slid open. Roxie's legs shook. "The couch." She wouldn't make it much farther without dumping Liam and herself on the floor, and she wanted to look at the wound. They flipped him to the couch, and she crouched. "Get me gauze!"

Maybe they had quick clot also. She tore open Liam's shirt and probed the wound. Concerned voices came from behind her.

"I can call the doctor. See how far away he is."

"Or an ambulance."

Roxie tuned them out as she leaned down and pushed Liam's hip up to peer on the other side. No entry or exit. "It's not bad. It's a graze."

She had to check for a wound anywhere else, or a head injury. She felt his skull with both hands, and the back of his head felt wet. Her fingertips bloody.

She said, "An ambulance would be good. He might have a concussion."

Liam's eyes flew open, and he grabbed her elbows.

"Whoa. Easy."

He blinked at her.

"Just me."

He sucked in a breath. "The Hummer?"

"Took off. You came to the right place since it seems Vanguard just saved your butt." She grinned.

"My hero." He grinned back, his eyes a little glassy.

"You hit your head. Nonsense is understandable."

He lay back and groaned.

"We're getting an ambulance."

He shook his head and didn't manage to hide a wince. "Ice pack."

"And that quick clotting stuff." Someone handed Roxie the medical bag. "Let's see here." She cracked an ice pack so it started cooling down and gave it to him. He held it to the back of his head and sat up.

Groaned.

"Go slow. And no standing for a while." She reached for his graze with a bandage covered in powder that would stop the steady leak.

"Did you rip my shirt?"

Someone behind her snickered.

"I like this shirt!" He gaped at her.

"I'll get you a new one."

He made a face an awful lot like a little kid pout.

She pressed the gauze to his graze and pushed hard, holding it in place per the instructions. He hissed, and she said, "Sorry."

He eyed her, then he glanced over her shoulder. "Did she drag me out of the car on her own?"

Someone said, "Yes, but the rest of us helped get you in."

Liam brushed hair back from her face gently, looking like he wanted to kiss her. *Danger.* He shouldn't bend, and they had an audience, but neither of those were the reasons why a kiss was a bad idea—the reason she needed to focus on.

"These are agents with the Northwest Counter-Terrorism Taskforce." A change of topic was a *great* idea. "Special Agent Dakota Pierce, Homeland Security, and her partner, who is also her husband, DEA Special Agent Josh Weber. The German shepherd is his K-9, Neema."

Liam frowned. "Never heard of you guys."

Dakota laughed. "That's how we like it." She reached over and shook Liam's hand over Roxie's shoulder. "Nice to meet you."

Liam glanced at Roxie. She nodded because he'd realized what she had—that these people's lives made no sense because what task force was set up like theirs? But they seemed nice. Like they wanted to do good in the world. Dakota ran the team. They had a few more team members who hadn't come to meet with Clare. Roxie couldn't remember the rest of it.

She'd tried to ignore his working dog, but who could? Dogs were the best, and this one was friendly. *Neema.*

"I'm Josh."

Liam shook his hand. "Sergeant O'Connell, Benson PD."

"Didn't you call your department for backup when you realized you were being shot at?"

Liam nodded, relaying a story about being told his badge number didn't exist.

Roxie's finger slipped off the tape she was using to hold down the bandage. "Are you kidding me?"

"I know." He squeezed her arm. "I'll get to the bottom of it, don't worry. But I got hung out to dry just now. It's only by the grace of God that I was close to you guys so I could get some help."

"Good." She didn't want him in danger anywhere except where she could get to him.

He got that look again, like he wanted to kiss her.

Clare said, "I'll call Gage."

Roxie stared at Liam. "They're going to answer for that. You could've died today." *Right in front of me.*

The group of people started to dissipate, moving away. Roxie didn't let go of the hard press of her lips, keeping her mouth closed so she didn't slip and let him know how she felt about him.

Liam shifted toward her.

She started to object. He needed to sit still!

Before she could blink, he pressed his lips to hers.

TWENTY-NINE

Liam lingered for a second, taking his time because he wanted to but also making it light and easy for Roxie. The last thing he wanted was to put pressure on her that she didn't need right now—or ever, really.

He was vaguely aware everyone had backed off and was talking in the corner of the lobby. Less aware than he was about the pounding in the back of his head, but when he finally had what he wanted, the discomfort didn't matter. He was resolute in his focus.

Roxie was what he wanted.

She shifted slightly, holding back. Liam broke off at her signal and held her gaze for a second, loving the way she looked a little surprised and a whole lot flushed. "That wasn't supposed to happen."

"I don't know about that." He felt a slight smile tug at his lips.

She frowned and sat back, picking up gauze packets and tossing them in the tiny wicker wastebasket at the end of the couch. When she returned, he clasped her hand and tugged her beside him. He probably looked like a sorry sight with his ripped shirt and bleeding head.

Still, he needed to say, "Whatever happens, I want you there with me."

She looked over at her colleagues and those two federal agents, then looked at him. "It's not up to you. It's my choice where I am and what I do."

"I'm not going anywhere." He leaned over even though it didn't feel good, but it was worth it for the sake of stealing another soft kiss. "Take as much time as you need."

She sighed, like maybe that wasn't a good thing. "You're delirious. It's the head injury talking."

He'd been injured before. He wasn't so worried, but he also wasn't going to say that he was fine. "Pupils?" He turned to her.

"You have your mother's eyes."

Liam wasn't sure that was a good thing.

"They're normal size, but that isn't always an indication of no concussion. You still need an ambulance."

With what had happened? He wasn't prepared to rely on emergency services right now. His stomach cramped because he didn't want to think about how it felt a lot like having SWAT taken away from him. Losing family. People he should've been able to rely on and count on. He needed a moment to be in denial before he got angry that he had to grieve the loss of what he should've had—backup.

Across the lobby, it looked like Clare wanted to come over and talk to them.

Roxie said, "I don't want to think that you might be another terrible decision."

He lifted a finger to hold off Clare, then said to Roxie, "I'm not. You can trust me."

"With my track record?" Roxie winced. "I want to trust that you'll be worth the risk."

And he was happy to prove to her that he would be. Any time she needed the reassurance, and even when she didn't. "Are you maybe willing to trust God?"

She gave him a soft smile. "I figured I should because it couldn't be worse than anything else I've tried."

He smiled. "Ask me any questions you have, but it's between you and Him. If you ask for help, He'll show up. Anything. Wisdom. Truth. Strength. Peace. Hope you can trust in because it's not wishful thinking. I haven't been the best example of a Christian lately, but I'll help if I can. We're all on the same journey."

Roxie's expression shifted to a thoughtful one. She was considering it, and for right now, that might be enough.

Clare came over with two bottled waters and handed them to Liam and Roxie. "Briefing?"

"Yes." He didn't nod. "And some pain pills."

She handed him a small white bottle of over the counter meds. Liam knocked a few back with half the bottle of water. Clare sat across from them in the corner chair. "Of the three names you gave me, one is viable as Roxie's stalker."

He felt her tense and reached to hold her hand.

Clare continued, "He was already on my radar, so it was good to have confirmation." The two federal agents wandered over to listen, and the dog lay down by the man's foot. The woman was Native American, and the guy was Caucasian. Both wore simple wedding bands, and they stood together in a way that indicated their comfort with each other.

"My guys haven't been able to locate him," Clare said. "Credit card is dark—his and Mark's that he was using. He dropped off socials nearly two years ago. We found a message from a concerned relative about the dangers of plastic surgery."

Liam frowned.

"He disappeared. Went off grid."

"And made himself look like Mark." Liam winced.

Roxie shifted, perched on the edge of the couch. "Who?"

Clare said, "Mark had a younger brother. Brad."

Roxie turned to Liam. "We should be talking about who just tried to kill you."

"Sure." Liam gently squeezed her hand. "But let's solve your problem at the same time."

Besides, thinking about how he'd been blackballed by officers in the department tore him up inside. He'd been targeted—with help from those gunmen, whoever they had been. Hired to attack a cop and most likely paid well. A lot of criminals would jump at the chance for that payday.

Sure, it could have been a clerical error. A simple mistake. But not likely.

The female federal agent looked at her partner-husband. "I like both of them."

He gave her an indulgent smile in response.

"What about Liam?" Roxie wasn't going to let the danger to him go.

His heart squeezed in his chest. She was invested in his well-being—which meant she cared about him.

Clare nodded. "Simon found the names of the two officers who showed up at the house where you and Peter were talking to the accountant's mother—"

"I asked about Liam." She didn't sound like she was being short with her boss, but her tone was clipped.

"It's connected," Clare said. "They're on the payroll at the Hurstwhile Center as security guards."

Liam didn't see much wrong with that. "A lot of cops have

second jobs to pay the bills." What he should be doing right now was confirming whether Raphi really had met with a guy at the jail. "That doesn't necessarily mean anything."

Even as he said it, his mind rolled around the implications. The accountant connected Hurstwhile to the Russians. Now the police were also connected? Too many coincidences?

Clare said, "Turnbull is also on the list."

Liam's stomach clenched. "I never completely believed what he said happened to my father." The story had been a little too simple, and when an officer lost their life in the heat of the moment, things were never clean-cut.

Not like that.

"Here's what we're going to do." Clare glanced at the door. Through the glass, he spotted the SWAT truck pull up. "Gage and the boys are going to take you back to work, and you're all going to pretend it's business as usual. Meanwhile, I'm going to tear apart the lives of a handful of cops and find any indication, if it exists, that they are either in something together, on the take, or part of a conspiracy."

Liam blew out a breath. "This wasn't how I thought this would go."

Clare said, "Your father wasn't dirty. He was the first one I looked at. There is not one single indication in any part of his life that he was connected or actively covering anything up. Nothing."

Liam let out a breath that felt like he'd been holding it for ten years. "Thank you."

Clare nodded.

The doors slid open, and the guys strode in.

"I filled them in," Clare said. "And I need to go check in with my people collecting evidence so we can find those people who came here and shot at one of *my* friends." She got up and walked away, followed by the two feds and the police dog.

Gage headed for her while Blake and Jasper came toward him. Roxie and Liam both stood.

Liam asked them, "You guys ever heard of a Northwest Counter-Terrorism Taskforce?"

Blake frowned. "Sounds cool, but is it a thing?"

Jasper scratched at his jaw. "My dad had something going on with them a year or so back. They're renegades, but they're good people."

Huh.

Roxie squeezed his hand. "I should get to work. Please have a doctor look at you."

He wasn't prepared to commit to that. "Be careful."

"I should say the same to you." To his surprise, she lifted up on the balls of her feet and kissed his cheek. Then she was gone.

"Back to work?" Jasper turned for the door. "This has been an eventful morning training exercise."

"Sure has," Blake said.

Liam rounded the coffee table and caught up to them. "I'll need an ice pack."

"That's cause you're old." Jasper offered over his shoulder.

"And wise." Liam cuffed him on the back of the head. "So don't you forget it."

Things might be crazy, but he still had his brothers in SWAT. Now he just might have Roxie as well.

It was time to settle an old score.

THIRTY

Roxie set her laptop on the conference room table. Peter stood by the whiteboard, and Bob shut the door behind him as he came in. They seemed to want to ask her about Liam and what had happened—in front of everyone—but they didn't. And she loved them all the more for it, knowing they were respecting her decision not to bring it up.

The fact was her head still spun.

What with the arrival of two federal agents and their dog, and the closed door meeting they'd had with Clare and Bob. Then the shoot-out out front and believing for a moment he might be dead. The call had come through the intercom that rang in every room in the whole building: Incoming. Police officer in danger. They'd run out, along with everyone else who wanted the chance to get in a firefight.

They were a strange breed, these operators. The kind of people who ran toward danger, not away from it. She was grateful to find others like her outside of the Marines. It made her feel a little less like an oddity in a world that people respected but didn't really understand.

"Ready?" Peter tapped the whiteboard marker on his other hand. The guy hadn't lost his tension since they'd been outside, but they'd worked together well out there. He was new and had less training than her, but she was rusty these days and needed to get back into it. They could spend some time upstairs, running through drills so they got really in sync.

Assuming that this thing became a more permanent position.

Did she want to stay where Liam was after this was over? After "Mark" was arrested or dead? Roxie gave herself a second to absorb it. "This is…" She couldn't believe what they'd found. "I'm not crazy."

Peter's smile softened. The kid was young but a good man already and someone she trusted. Why was it necessary for her to keep reminding herself of that? She could trust the people around her. Colleagues, and friends. Liam and the guys he worked with in SWAT.

She had a support system here. Something she hadn't had in a long time—but which she couldn't help being grateful for. *Is that Your doing, God? If so, thank You. Help me work out this thing with Liam so I can get to a place where I'm not scared anymore.*

Bob came over to Peter and sank into a leather chair. "Run it down for me."

Peter said, "Bottom line, Clare was right—no surprise there. It looks like when Mark died, Brad assumed his life, or at least his appearance and his credit cards, and decided to torment Roxie."

What she needed to know was where it would stop. And how soon that was going to occur. Liam might have been the catalyst for the things that had happened recently, but surely, Brad couldn't do this forever. He must have a plan to finish it, finally.

No matter how it ended, at least it would be over.

Roxie had found a picture of the brothers as kids in Mark's house long ago. Why hadn't she remembered that? She'd been so traumatized by what was happening, thinking she was seeing a dead man, that she hadn't recalled it until Peter showed her a picture of Brad Mills. Even without plastic surgery, they'd resembled each other.

At this point, she'd rather think about Liam and his kisses. Better than a man who'd painted a target on her and Liam. Or maybe the Northwest Counter-Terrorism people and what they might be doing here.

But if she didn't face this, then she would have to live with it forever, like a symptom of a disease, ignored and never treated.

Bob grunted. "How do we find and catch this guy?"

Roxie nearly smiled. It was sweet of Bob to be offended on her behalf.

"What?" Bob frowned at her.

"You care about me."

"I have a daughter. She's tough like you. An FBI agent." He shrugged. "Doesn't mean I wouldn't kick in doors and have words with someone who was harassing her. And if they continued?" He shook his head, a dark look in his eyes. "I'm not a cop anymore. I'm a convicted criminal. It's not like anyone would be surprised by what I'd do."

Roxie set both palms on the table and leaned forward. "Don't kill someone on my behalf." There were ways to end a life that were legal, so it didn't count if he had to protect himself or someone else by taking out Brad. They all knew that. But murder? She wouldn't be the reason his daughter would have to visit him in prison for the rest of his life.

Bob shot her a look like, *I do what I want.*

"Let's try to take care of this without any of us getting arrested, okay?"

Peter grinned. "I like a challenge."

Bob said, "So, who is this dirtbag?"

Roxie found the police file they'd requested from Seattle PD. "Brad Mills was questioned in the disappearance of Mark's wife. Though he was never officially arrested, they talked to him at length. A friend of his provided an alibi, and they had to drop it for lack of evidence of any other possibilities."

It wasn't much, but it also wasn't nothing.

If the police there had reason to talk to him, that meant he'd been under suspicion. She was waiting for one of the officers to get her message and then call her back so she could ask why they suspected him. She needed to hear it right from the officer rather than read into what he wasn't saying in this report.

"He also had a juvenile record we got into," Peter said. "He set a fire in a shed at the high school and did some time in youth detention with mandatory therapy afterward. They tried a brand-new, innovative program designed to steer him onto a better path." He made a face. "I'm not sure it worked."

Bob snorted. "And we have reason to believe he's local right now? Any idea where to find him?"

Roxie said, "There are no properties listed under his name or his brother's, rented or owned. No vehicle registered to him. His driver's license is valid, but we have no idea how he's getting around."

"And you were hit by that Hummer when you were in Liam's truck?" Bob asked.

She nodded. "I have to conclude that since it's the most straightforward answer. Until we can confirm paint transfer from the truck to the same vehicle that pulled up outside, it's not definitive."

At this point, it was a mystery how it all connected.

Maybe they'd thought she was Liam in his truck. Maybe Brad had hired those people to try and kill her, and then Liam. But when his attack connected—most likely—to dirty cops, then she had to wonder if Brad might not be connected to that as well.

"We found a link between Brad and Matvei Obolensky, the old guy who died in the limo bombing," Peter said.

Bob nodded.

Roxie pushed away the mental image of Tessa looking like she'd been dragged across asphalt. Her friend, and K-9 trainer, had soldiered on the way Roxie was trying to do. Tessa had stayed standing, holding firm when all kinds of craziness exploded around her.

If only Roxie could have half of that class in the face of all this.

Bob said, "What's the connection between Brad and the Russians?"

Peter had that information. "Looks like he did some work in one of their clubs after high school. Bouncer, then bartender. That kind of thing. He could've been pulled in on the family stuff as well. It's a short step to being one of the guys that goes out and breaks the legs of people who won't pay."

"But we can't prove that," Roxie pointed out. Her laptop messenger app for their internal network pinged. "Simon has something. Hang on." She clicked it. "Looks like after Mark went missing, he rented out the house they shared fully furnished. The family still owns it since Mark's property went to his brother."

"Whose name is the house in?" Bob asked.

Roxie shook her head. "Looks like it was still listed under the wife. Her family is going to court to get it turned over to them. It's not clear who is living there, but it's about half an hour away."

"Take a team." Bob stood, glancing between them. "Go check it out. We need to find this guy."

THIRTY-ONE

The whole SWAT team had been on eggshells all afternoon. Now, in their van, Jasper leaned forward and patted Liam's shoulder. "You good?"

They'd agreed it would look odd if he wasn't driving since he was the only one who had ever driven this particular vehicle. "Yeah. My side doesn't hurt too bad."

"No double vision?"

The bleeding on the back of his head hadn't lasted long. They'd suggested figuring out what it was on Gage's center console that he'd hit, but this was time to work, not think about what had happened. "I'm good."

"Let's just get to my house, yeah?" Gage sat in the passenger seat. He hadn't rolled out with them much in the last couple of months, so having him here was good. Nostalgic.

"You think breaking up SWAT back to part-time is because of what's going on?"

Gage said, "Russ will tell us. He wouldn't have signed off on something that was about targeting you and hamstringing your career."

"I just don't want you guys to get caught in the dragnet."

His brothers on SWAT deserved to move to better positions. He prayed about that now—and about everything else. He'd spoken to his mom this afternoon and cleared the air about her hiring Vanguard. He wasn't mad about it now that he'd heard how unsettled she'd been for years.

She'd either kept it from him so he wouldn't worry, since there hadn't been anything he could do without damaging his career, or he hadn't listened when she'd spoken about it.

He probably got his need to safeguard the people in his life from her. She hadn't wanted him to be affected by her worry if the accusation came to nothing. Turned out hiring Vanguard was a good idea.

He glanced over at Gage. "I get it."

"You mean, why you hesitated to tell them things were changing?"

He nodded.

"So tell me what you figured out."

"I found something with you guys." He glanced at the rearview, then at the lieutenant. "A family like what I had in the Marines." Even if a lot of that had been his connection with Roxie. "Something I didn't want to lose."

Gage reached over and squeezed his shoulder. "Things will change, but we aren't going anywhere."

Jasper sniffed. "He loves us, Blake. He really loves us."

"Yeah," Liam said. "Like the two irritating little brothers I never knew I needed." He had two brothers, and these guys in the vehicle were closer to him than them. Sometimes life just worked out that way. He should call Rory and check in since it had been a while.

Blake chuckled. "I have a few feelers out, but I got a visit from McCauley."

"Yeah?" Gage turned. Captain McCauley was his half-brother, something Gage had only found out recently. He was also over the major crimes detective squad.

Liam had figured one of them would. Blake and Jasper would end up in solid positions—especially with brass that they all respected headhunting them.

"What about you, Jas?" He pulled the vehicle up to the curb in front of the house where Gage lived with Clare. "What's on the horizon for you once you make detective?" He shut off the engine and turned to his friend.

Jasper didn't speak right away. Was that what he wanted? Finally, Jasper said, "Not sure. I have an idea about something else even, but I need to chat with a couple of people first. See what they think."

He wanted to keep things close to his vest? That was a good idea if he wasn't sure what the outcome would be.

"Good for you." Liam nodded. "Whatever it is, we're behind you one hundred percent." Jasper had to know that. His father might be an aloof state senator who thought affection meant buying Jasper another sports car, but they could be there for him.

"Good." Gage reached for his door. "Now that we're done with the lovefest, let's go."

Liam got out, scanning the street just in case those guys in the Hummer showed up again. By the sound of it, the Vanguard employees had shot one and perhaps wounded a couple more before the Hummer fled the scene.

A silver sedan in the drive didn't belong to anyone he knew.

Gage went in first, calling out, "Honey, we're home!"

Clare crossed the expansive living room. "I see you brought the kids with you." She kissed her husband.

Liam nodded. Clare assessed him, then looked at Blake and Jasper. Behind her, he saw the living room was full of people. Two female FBI agents chatted with Russ. The male Northwest Counter-Whatever guy stood with his arms folded, the dog at his feet. The female Homeland Security agent, Special Agent Dakota Pierce, strode in from the direction of the restroom, wearing her clothes from earlier but carrying a pair of gold heels and a piece of material that couldn't possibly be big enough to be a dress.

The male special agent, Josh Weber, said, "Shame. I liked that outfit."

She shoved his shoulder, then stuffed the clothes into a duffel on the floor.

"Something happening we need to know about?" Liam glanced around in time to see Russ Franklin—the police commissioner—walk in with a mug.

The commissioner lifted his mug in a salute, apparently making himself comfortable.

Clare said, "You've walked into a joint operation, with private support."

"Meaning?" Liam shoved Blake and Jasper in, and they all sat.

"Meaning I spent the last hour at a sports bar easing up to Lieutenant Turnbull and settling in," Dakota said as she sat beside her husband. "Asking about his life and getting him sauced enough to say things he wouldn't have otherwise."

"He's on the take?" Liam's brows rose. "I looked into him. Apart from a cushy post and a cupcake level of responsibility, I couldn't find anything untoward."

"It's all in his wife's name," Clare said.

Dakota nodded. "He claims she made a bunch of money a few years ago by investing in some multilevel marketing scheme."

The same one as the guy in prison Morgan had talked to? He'd called the jail earlier about the fact he'd been notified

Raphi was there. No one had a clue what he was talking about. So the whole thing had been a hoax to get him out and away from the department so that the Hummer of gunmen and their friends could begin their attack.

Liam said, "You went undercover?"

"He doesn't know me." Dakota shrugged.

"And she has better legs than me." Her husband grinned.

Jasper chuckled.

Liam went to scratch the back of his head, but he stopped short because it was still tender. "So, he has money, but he has an explanation for it."

"The company folded." Clare shook her head. "Before his wife could've worked with them."

It was one of the two female FBI agents in the room who said, "And he has a Corvette, a lake house, and both of his kids go to private school." Addie Franklin was Russ's niece. "Though, the kids are on scholarship this year. The Corvette is getting old. House needs updating. The money he got is running out."

The other agent was Bob's daughter. Stella said, "We might be able to lean on him. Get Dakota to dangle some bait." Stella grinned. "She's pretty good at that."

Dakota grinned as well. "I'm in. This is fun."

Josh said, "As if we don't have enough open cases of our own."

Speaking of cases, why were they in town meeting with Clare anyway? "Does one of them involve Vanguard?"

Dakota tipped her head to the side. "I'll fill you in after your thing is wrapped up, yeah?"

Liam nodded. "I would like to get to the bottom of this. Dirty cops, payouts. My father's death."

Clare glanced at Gage when he slid his arm around her. "My people discovered a connection between the Russian family you're going after, the Hurstwhile Center, and Roxie's...you know. Brad Mills."

Liam nodded. "The Russians are behind what the center is doing and the dirty cops, right?"

Clare shrugged. "We can't prove who the instigator is."

"We need to bring down Raphi Obolensky. Then, this empire ends." It had cost too much already.

Blake squeezed his shoulder. "And get this Brad guy in the process."

That sounded great. "Where is Roxie?" She had been working this afternoon when he'd texted, following a lead.

"Trying to get a location on Brad." Clare lifted a hand. "She has a team for protection."

Wherever she was, it was good to know she was being safeguarded. Meanwhile, it seemed like he'd been handed the chance to avenge his father's death.

Liam glanced around. "Let's make a plan."

THIRTY-TWO

Roxie stared at the screen of the laptop on the trunk of the Toyota. The breeze whipped her hair across her face, so she tucked it back behind her ear. She needed to redo her ponytail but wanted to get into the house more.

Peter navigated the drone through the house, clearing rooms without putting anyone in danger if Brad was hiding in the house. A drone with video wouldn't see inside closed closets, but this one had an infrared camera, so they'd see any heat signatures inside. The house was empty as far as they could see. "Okay, that's the last one." He stepped back. "I'll get the drone out, and we can go in."

Roxie stepped back from the trunk and slipped her earpiece in. "On it." She headed for the others by their SUV who were already gearing up. "We're a go. House is empty."

There were four others with them. Usually, when they did something like this, it would be just her and Peter. These Vanguard employees were here to protect her.

One studied her, a guy who just came off a personal

protection job for a singer in Tennessee. "Maybe you should wear a helmet."

Roxie said, "If you're worried about a sniper, I should have put it on before I got out of the car." She turned away. She was all for exercising reasonable caution, but full body armor would only slow her down and leave her without the range of motion she needed when she came face-to-face with him again.

Brad.

Not Mark.

Her heart and mind were still having trouble processing that it wasn't the man who had tormented her and mixed up her thoughts for so long. Only the benefit of hindsight let her look at it, and she still wasn't far enough out of it for her mind to have things completely straight.

One day she would get to the point where she would wonder how she ever could have believed what Mark told her. How she had been so thoroughly sucked in and manipulated. It was easier to see how much she'd been deceived from the outside looking in, but in the middle of it, she had succumbed. Things had seemed to make sense that now didn't.

"You good?" Peter didn't look up.

She heard the whir of the drone coming down the side of the house. "Just thinking."

He landed the drone on the lid of the trunk and glanced over. "Don't think too much. Time to work."

He'd told her how he'd gone through a lot in his youth, and even recently. "You see the company shrink, right?"

He nodded, a blank look settling over his face. "Clare made it mandatory when she pulled us into Vanguard for community service. I picked it back up for a few sessions recently, but I needed less than I thought I did."

"I might make an appointment."

"It's a good idea."

"I lived at the Ridgeman Center in Last Chance County for a few weeks after…" She touched the scar on the side of her face. "But I think I need to pick it back up, like you did."

Peter said, "They do premarital counseling as well, if you want."

Roxie frowned so hard it sparked pain in her temples. "What?"

"In case." He shrugged, a knowing look in his eyes.

"Can we break and enter into this house already?" That would be preferable to this conversation. Liam might be another topic to bring up during a counseling session. That was all for right now, as far as she was concerned.

Peter chuckled. "Just you wait."

Roxie went to the door, but one of the guys stepped in first. They'd picked the lock on the front door half an hour ago to let the drone in, so if there had been a security system, the police would have shown up. Occasionally, Vanguard let the police know they were on an operation. Given the current climate with Liam, she'd said a prayer of thanks that they were farther out of Benson in a secluded cul-de-sac.

The guy behind her tapped her shoulder.

Roxie stepped in with the cover of someone behind her back. They searched the ground level and found a door to a basement. "Yay, I love basements."

Peter chuckled behind her. "I can go first."

"I've got it." She headed down steep wooden stairs, one hand on the ceiling above her that was low enough she had to duck her head. "Watch your step."

"Yep."

She didn't look back, just scanned the basement. An ancient washer and dryer, on top of which was a laundry basket overflowing with dark-colored clothes. "We need to search that." She pointed at it, more interested in the shelving on the other side. Mark had a similar setup in the garage of his house.

It had never been hers, but such was the nature of their relationship. She hadn't owned anything—not even her sense of self.

She helped Peter clear every corner, cupboard, and place where someone could hide. Then she stowed her weapon and headed for the shelves.

Peter said, "What is it?"

She couldn't have articulated it if she tried. "Can you check those clothes? Maybe there's evidence if he hasn't washed them yet."

"On it." Peter crossed the room.

Roxie pulled a storage bin out, far enough that she could flip the lid. Winter gear, snow pants, and a pair of boots. The one beside it had a bunch of women's clothes. She rummaged inside but found nothing between the fabric or at the bottom.

She continued down the line, checking each one.

Finally she hit on something interesting when she found a box tucked behind another one. "Here we go."

She slid the box onto the floor and flipped the lid off.

"I've got trace evidence on these clothes," Peter said. "Blood and dirt. I'm not going to touch anything else. I'll call Clare and let her know."

She nodded, her focus on the stack of books inside, along with some old photo albums. Roxie started to go through them. Peter knelt by her and did the same.

She said, "This one is a ledger."

"This is a photo album but look." He showed her a picture.

"That isn't a vacation photo." If it was, it would have been of Mark and the woman he'd married years ago. "That looks like a driver's license photo." Beside it was a cutout of a newspaper article, a local man who'd had a seizure at a baseball game. "A memento?"

"Looks like it." Peter flipped the page. "It's full of them. Copies of photos, and printouts of articles. Each one is a death, by many different means. Accidents, medical tragedies, and vehicle crashes. One missing person discovered dead in a river after days of dredging by rescue crews."

Roxie shook her head. "That's crazy. He did all that?"

"Look." Peter showed her a newspaper article about a limo bombing that had killed a man.

"Was it Brad or Mark, though?" One of them had kept a record of random deaths. Or were they? "Recording a completed job."

"Maybe that's what one of these ledgers is. Someone hired him to do jobs like this, and he got away with them."

"But who hired him?"

Peter nodded. "All good questions we need to figure out the answers to. Like why you'd hide something sensitive here instead of in a better place."

"It's in plain sight."

A thunder of footsteps drew her attention to the stairs where two of the men came down. "You guys find something?"

Peter explained what they thought it might be. "How about you?"

"Evidence he's been making bombs."

Roxie didn't even touch that. "Do we know for sure Brad was living here recently? It's his stuff?"

Her colleague nodded. "And from what we can see, he's got enough up there that he made at least one explosive device recently."

Roxie set the album in the storage bin and stood. "Any idea where?"

They needed to find him now *and* stop whatever plan he had in motion.

Her colleague shook his head. "No maps, papers, or computer. No tablet or phone. Nothing upstairs that would give us a clue where he plans to deploy the device."

"But you did find something." She started toward the stairs.

He held up his hand. "You won't be looking at it. We're documenting what we've found, and it will be in the mission report."

"What is it?" Her body flushed and then went cold.

"He dislikes you, and that feeling is clearly displayed in a collage of photographs, not only of you but several people you know. Clare can read my final report, and we'll be ensuring those people are safeguarded." He held her stare with a steady gaze. "This is good. We can develop intel from this."

Roxie blew out a breath, trying to let that settle in. She managed to nod.

Peter squeezed her shoulder.

"I need to make some calls." She balled her hands into fists. The people on the collage deserved to know now. "But you need to tell me who to check in with."

He acquiesced, saying, "Call your roommate. She's featured prominently."

Roxie strode up the stairs toward the front door but didn't go outside. She listened to her phone ring against her ear. And ring.

And ring.

"Destiny. Pick up."

THIRTY-THREE

L iam pulled the SWAT van over to the curb outside Destiny's townhome. At the same time, two other vehicles—a Toyota and an SUV—showed up. Blake jumped out before Liam brought the van to a complete stop.

Liam watched for Roxie and saw how her colleagues moved around her like a protective detail. That alone made him feel better. The rest of what was happening, not so much.

He jumped down and slammed the door, already geared up. He jogged over and met Peter at the front walk while the rest of them headed inside. Roxie ran to the house before he could say anything to her. "What happened?"

"We don't know." Peter headed for the house, and Liam jogged beside him.

As much as he would've liked to talk to Roxie, this was about Destiny's well-being and her location. She would be focused on finding her friend. "Has anyone spoken to Destiny?"

Peter shook his head. "She hasn't answered her phone. We located her GPS, and it has her device here."

"Blake did the same." Not because they thought they'd get

a different answer, but his buddy hadn't known what else to do on the way over.

They reached the door right as Roxie came back to it. "She isn't here." Her face pale, she bit her lip.

Liam slid his arm around her and stepped inside, drawing her into a hug. He kissed her forehead. "We'll find her." Then just as quickly, he let go and kept moving. "Come farther inside." The last thing he wanted was for Roxie to be exposed at the door and either go missing like Destiny or worse. "Everyone on me!" He called the words out, sharp and loud.

When the Vanguard operatives and his SWAT guys swarmed back into the living room, Liam glanced at his lieutenant and got a nod. He recognized one of the Vanguard guys. "Jasper, take Collins and go do a perimeter walk. Figure out how they got in and out." The front door had been closed when they got here.

He turned to Blake. "Who was bringing her home from Backdraft?"

The officer pulled his phone. "I messaged the bartender I know, and he said Conrad left to drive Destiny home, and he was going to stay with her until Vanguard got here."

Roxie let out a tiny mew.

He didn't glance at her. The last thing she needed right now was attention drawn to her. Instead, he said to Jasper, "I'll call Conrad. You take a look outside."

They headed for the door.

Liam pulled out his phone. "Everyone else, knock on the neighbors' doors. Find out if anyone saw anything." They all started to move. "Roxie, stay with me."

Even Gage headed out to knock on neighbors' doors.

"Why do I need to stay?" Her words quivered when she spoke, but she held it together.

"I don't want you exposed or out of sight."

"So I have to stay where you can see me, like a little kid."

He took a step closer to her, noting that she hung back. "This is about finding Destiny. It's why we're all here." And he needed to call Conrad to see where his brother was. "But I don't want to risk anything happening to you as well."

She pulled back a little. "I'm good. I don't need babysitting or special favors."

That determined look in her eye scared him as much as it made him proud that she was ready to fight back. The worry was that she was looking for a fight. Especially now that her friend was missing.

He called his brother's number.

The call connected, and he heard, "Sarge?"

"Jasper? Where are you?" He strode to the door and stepped out, Roxie with him.

"South side street. Hurry." Jasper hung up.

Roxie ran beside him, double-time to the south side where they turned the corner, and he spotted Jasper and Collins kneeling. Conrad lay on the ground on his back.

"What happened?" Liam raced to them.

Collins glanced over. "Looks like he got hit over the head."

Jasper dug in one of his pouches and produced gauze. "Ambulance is already en route."

"Copy that." He knelt in an open spot where he could see the now bloody gauze in Collins' fingers over the wound.

Roxie set her hand on the back of his neck, probably trying to infuse some solidarity into him. Her thumb brushed the spot on the back of his neck that had scabbed over since yesterday. He hadn't taken any pain meds, so a sharp stabbing sensation ricocheted from the back of his head.

He flinched and glanced at her, figuring she would recognize what happened, then looked back at his brother. Conrad's eyes fluttered open.

"Hey." Liam shifted so he'd be able to see his brother. "Hey, Con."

His brother frowned. "What happened?" The words weren't too slurred, and his eyes looked pretty clear.

"You've got that O'Connell hard head like me." He leaned down close. "I need you to tell me where Destiny is. What happened?"

Conrad blinked, a slow closing and opening of his eyes. "Destiny."

"Yep. What happened?" He gave his brother a second to process the question and get his thoughts together. He could hear sirens in the distance, the only reason he managed to hold it together.

Destiny was out there somewhere. But at least it wasn't Roxie—though, that was a small comfort. He would lose it if anything happened to Blake's sweet younger sister.

Conrad managed to say, "He jumped me."

"Did you see his face?"

Conrad winced. "She screamed."

"Did he take her?" Destiny wasn't here. Was she still alive?

Conrad's gaze moved, as though searching for her.

"You didn't see him take her?"

Conrad's eyes filled with moisture. He hissed out a breath.

"I know. It hurts, but we're going to get you to the hospital, okay? I'll call Mom. Everything will be fine." Liam held his brother's hand up in the middle of his chest. "Just hang on, okay?"

Conrad blinked.

"Did you see his car?"

"Black. Or blue." Conrad's voice was starting to slur. He was losing consciousness. "Where..."

The EMTs pulled up. There were calls to make once Conrad was on his way to the hospital. People who needed to gather to hear the news, and others who would want to activate a prayer chain to cover the prognosis with requests to God.

Liam got out of the way. Roxie was no longer beside him. "Roxie!"

"I think she went back to the house with Collins." Jasper rose to his feet.

Liam hadn't even noticed them leaving. "I need to..." He didn't know what to do first. He turned to the street where he'd come from, then back in time to see the EMTs lift his brother onto their stretcher.

"Are you following us, Sarge?"

He shook his head. "I'll have his wife and my mom meet you at the hospital."

He needed to help find Destiny.

Liam and Jasper jogged back to the townhouse, where the others were gathered in front. Roxie stood by Peter, clearly comfortable in his sphere. She needed a support system that included all kinds of people, but if only it could be him most of the time—when either of them wasn't working. If they worked together full-time he could watch her back, which was probably what those two married Northwest Counter-Terrorism agents did.

But that was an idea for the future. Not right now, when she would barely look at him.

He strode up to the group. "What's the word on witnesses?"

Blake turned to him. "We've got a make and model of the vehicle and a partial license plate."

That was good. "What about a description?"

Blake nodded. "Two guys, both dark-haired. Younger." So,

not the cops who'd harassed Peter and Roxie, then. "They stuffed her in the trunk." Blake's voice broke on that last word.

Liam held his friend's gaze. "If they wanted to kill her, they'd have done it. They took her alive."

Blake nodded. "I called in the vehicle information to get a BOLO out."

"I need to tell my mom what happened to Conrad. Then we can get to work." Liam tugged out his phone again and dialed his mom's number, hoping she would pick up, considering they'd aired out their issue and resolved it. "Come on."

The call connected, and all he heard was a male moan.

"Who is this?" Liam turned away from the group. "Who are you?"

"Bob Davis." He groaned.

The Vanguard department head was at his mom's house. "Bob, why are you answering my mom's phone?"

The older man moaned again. "She's... They took her."

"Who took her?"

"Two men." Bob cleared his throat. "They hit me and took your mom."

THIRTY-FOUR

Roxie took a step toward Liam but the cops with them swarmed around him, stepping between her and the man she cared about—loved, probably. Not that she would allow herself to contemplate it any more than that.

Not when she was the one who had moved away from him. Sought solace with a neutral party while she figured out everything she was feeling. Destiny was gone. His brother had been hurt. Now his mom was gone as well? What on earth was going on? His family was being targeted, but with all of that swirling around—all the fear and the confusion—she couldn't help but stare at how steady he was.

Like a redwood.

Or one of those trees in a river that grew despite what constantly hammered them. It survived, growing tall and strong through sheer determination.

He'd taken charge of the situation in her house when they had to search for Destiny and his brother. The sight of that much authority had scared her. Put her on edge. Mark would have used it to batter her psyche and get his way, making her believe that was what she wanted—or at least that she wanted the path of least resistance.

She still had to sort it all out in her head. Why get into another relationship and risk ending up in the same place?

Peter slung an arm around her shoulder and tugged her to his side. "We need to go see Bob."

She nodded.

"Hold up." Collins, the Vanguard agent she worked with, held up one hand. "Roxie goes with us. She's going to a safe house right now." He had his phone in his other hand. "Clare's orders."

Liam tugged her to him so fast she blinked, and her face smashed against the front of his vest. "Gotta go. Be safe."

The cops jogged away, continuing the search for two people now.

"I'm going to Bob." Peter shot her a look, almost pleading with her to understand. "I need to be there at the hospital."

She nodded. "Go."

If they weren't going to let her be in public, at least Peter would be there for their boss. Clearly, Peter thought of him more like a father. He'd told her about how his original father was an evil man, even before anyone else figured that out. Peter and Simon had kept their sister in the dark for years, safeguarding her belief in the man who'd raised them. When it came out that he was a criminal, they could no longer stop everything from coming to a head.

Even if they'd been working quietly on their own to take him down.

Now that he had Bob in his life, of course, he'd want to wait for word in the hospital.

But she didn't have the luxury.

She turned to Collins, already knowing the answer to her question. "I can't even go to the hospital?"

"I'll keep you apprised of what's happening." Collins didn't back down. "The ambulance just got to the house." He waved to their SUV, the only vehicle still there. "Let's go."

Roxie walked toward it. She'd prefer not to put anyone around her in danger if it came down to that. But then again, she also didn't want to sit somewhere doing nothing to help find Destiny—and now Liam's mom. She could pray and get some things straight, but in reality, all she would do was sit around thinking about her feelings for Liam.

He'd always carried that larger-than-life air around with him everywhere. Taking care of his brother, but also getting the information they needed.

More than one man had taken Destiny.

How many had taken Liam's mom?

She stopped at the door and looked at Collins, who was holding it open for her. Protecting her. "Why take the two of them?"

"Get in."

"Liam's mom, that's kind of understandable if dirty cops are trying to hit back at him for whatever he's getting close to. Or what *we're* getting close to."

He set his hand gently on her shoulder, like he was going to say something reassuring. Then he shoved her at the open door. "Get in, Roxie."

She caught herself and scrambled in. He slammed the door and went around to the other side, climbing in the back beside her. Another guy was in the front passenger seat. The driver threw it in gear and pulled out. If she hadn't seen them around the office, she might be worried right now.

"Safe house, huh?"

Collins typed on his phone. Probably updating Clare as to the fact they were mobile now.

None of them spoke to her.

"You guys must have a theory as to why they grabbed Blake's sister, Destiny. Sweetest woman you've ever met in your life, by the way. Don't let the pizza grill waitress thing fool you. She's got a heart as big as Alaska. She's going to Africa in the new year to do missions for six months. A woman like that could change the world."

Tears gathered in her eyes.

Collins said, "They have their jobs, we have ours. SWAT will find their sister."

She swiped at her cheeks, trying not to be obvious about it but not fooling anyone. "And Liam's mom."

"And their mom."

He was right. They did consider Destiny to be a sister to all of them. And Liam's mom was a lot like an honorary mom.

Someone Roxie would've liked to get to know. And still could, if she came through this.

Where were they?

God, You know. Are they together? That might be nice if they were in the same place and could comfort each other. *Keep them safe until they can be found.*

"Where are we headed?"

Collins glanced at her. "Depends on what you want to do."

If he'd have asked her then if she wanted to be kidnapped, she'd have said yes. Being there would mean she could help the two missing women get free. She glanced at him, unsure how to explain that without sounding insane.

"Do you want to end this?"

She stared at him. "What do you think?"

"I think you're a marine."

"I'm a lot of other things, too." A victim. A coward. A survivor.

"I know about those as well. Clare got me up to speed."

He paused for a split second. "So, what do you say, Marine? Want to end this, even if it means hanging you out like bait?"

She glanced over at him. "What do you think?"

He smiled, and she caught a flash of teeth in his grin. "Figured you'd say that." They pulled into a residential neighborhood. He started dragging stuff out of his pockets, all those little pouches on his belt. "That's why we're here."

He handed her a tiny penlight. Then, a palm-sized can of pepper spray, which she tucked up her sleeve. She put a pocketknife in her boot. He held up a button-sized medallion on a black cord. "Put this over your neck. It has a tracker."

She didn't hesitate. "You're really going to hang me out as bait? Clare approved it?"

"Clare approved a plan involving a highly skilled, 'prepared to use deadly force' operative as bait. You wanna be the vulnerable kind?"

"No."

He chuckled and pointed at the window. "That house over there. You remember that woman from the restaurant, the one having dinner with Liam? That's your in."

Or it was the end of the line for her.

Either way, this would be over.

"You think Destiny and Liam's mom are both there?"

Collins said, "Vanguard surveillance tracked the vehicles here. We've been keeping an eye on Karina in connection with Obolensky. We need someone on the inside, and the drone is too loud."

"Right." Roxie shoved the door open. "I've got my phone."

"Copy that. Simon already connected us."

She checked and spotted a message, then headed for the front door of the house with no idea what would greet her on the other side. An army? The one man in the world she was more afraid of than anything? Something in between?

Roxie walked up the drive toward the front door.

Behind her, down the street where they'd parked the SUV, a huge explosion ripped through the air. She twisted around in time to see the SUV launch into the air and flip over. A ball of fire erupted from under it.

The SUV slammed back to the ground.

Someone grabbed her.

Roxie screamed.

THIRTY-FIVE

"I guess Bob volunteered to *protect* your mom."

Liam spun around and got in Jasper's face, his hands balling into fists at his sides. "What did you just say?"

Fear flickered in Jasper's eyes, not that he had anything to be afraid of—except getting suspended by his sergeant.

Gage slapped a hand on the front of Liam's vest, keeping him where he was. "Easy."

"Dude. That's his mom." Blake was holding it together a whole lot better than Liam right now.

"We don't need to surmise why Bob was here." Gage folded his arms. "We need to confirm it was the same people that took both women."

"The two events happened close together in time." Liam had been thinking about this while also thinking about Roxie and where she might be. Why had there been that tension in her stance, and why had she put distance between them? "If they drove between, it could've been the same people. But what's the correlation between Destiny and Mom?"

Gage said, "You and Roxie."

"So am I the target or is she?" Liam frowned. "If it's dirty cops, then why take Destiny and make Roxie a part of it? And if it's Mark—Brad—then why involve my family?"

"Didn't Vanguard say they'd found some indication Brad was a hit man for hire, who'd kept a record of his kills?" Gage asked. "Maybe he worked for the Russians."

"That means you've got to connect the Russians and the dirty cops that work for Hurstwhile."

Blake's expression hardened. "Maybe the whole thing is connected. All of it. Everyone."

Gage's phone rang. Liam's started to vibrate in his pocket. Blake shifted, then Jasper, as though the same thing was happening to them.

The lieutenant said, "Let's go."

At the same time, Liam read the text on his watch. "Bomb detonation?" In a residential area?

They headed out the door of his mom's house, leaving the officers and crime scene techs to finish up. The evidence collected would seal the case for whoever had taken his mom. But he was going to be there when they found her, got her back, and cuffed the people who took her. Same with Destiny.

This wasn't going to end up a homicide investigation—not if he had anything to do with it.

Liam climbed into the driver's seat. "Where?"

Doors shut. Seat belts clicked in. Gage gave him the street address.

Liam hit the gas. "That's where Obolensky lives."

Ten minutes later, they pulled onto the street, into an ocean of blue and red flashing lights. Police cars. Fire trucks. The firefighters had their hose out already and were spraying the SUV down. An ambulance passed them. The sirens came on, and it headed in the direction of the hospital, moving fast.

"Roxie."

Gage reached over and squeezed his shoulder. "Park and let's go find her."

They piled out and jogged. She'd been headed for safety, so far as he knew. He ran for the closest firefighter and grabbed his turnout coat, spinning the guy around to get in his face. And got a Halligan bar pressed to his ribs—which he supposed was the firefighter equivalent of holding a gun on someone.

"How many people were in there?"

The guy blinked, and the Halligan lowered. "Step off."

Liam let go of him. "We've had two kidnappings today, and now this. How many people were in there?"

"Three guys. One dead, two critical already on their way to the hospital."

"And the woman who was in there?" Liam's stomach clenched. Where was Roxie?

The firefighter shook his head. "No female. Now back up and let us work."

Gage slapped a hand on his shoulder. "On me."

"What is it?" Liam spun as he asked the question.

"Neighbor reports that the woman went to the house before the SUV exploded. A car left shortly after." Gage pointed at the Obolensky family home. "She then asked us to make sure the street was completely cleaned because she's having a dinner party tonight."

Liam blinked.

"Let's go." Gage led the way, and they all jogged to the house, away from the first responders. The door to the house stood open. "On me."

They stacked up on the door, off to the side. Liam right behind Gage. Blake behind him. Jasper at the back. Gage stepped inside. Liam went right behind him and turned the other direction. They cleared the entryway. "Search the house."

Jasper went with Liam since they alternated. Just the way things played out. "Hey, I'm sorry about that comment about your mom and Bob. It was out of line."

Liam kept moving through the house. They headed upstairs. Gage and Blake would take the first floor. Liam scanned what he could see. Listened. Watched for any indication there was someone here, or that someone had been here—and what had happened. A million things, most of which was instinct that had been trained into him over and over again.

Liam said, "Let's just find them."

"We will. Don't worry about that, Sarge."

He wasn't. It was more about what condition he would find them in.

"I just need to say this."

He felt more than heard Jasper behind him.

Jasper spoke again. "I'm sorry, okay? I don't know what's up with me, and this isn't the time for it all to start leaking out."

"You've had a rough year." His friend had been strong-armed by his family into dumping his fiancée. Now what did he have except SWAT? Jasper's parents barely spoke to him. Too busy with state senate business and dinner parties in houses that looked a lot like this one. "We're good, Jas."

"Thanks. I appreciate it."

They cleared a couple of bedrooms and found a locked door. "Bathroom, you think?"

Jasper glanced around. "Or the closet."

In a house like this, it probably led through to an ornate bathroom. Liam lifted his foot and kicked the door open.

"You never let me do the cool stuff."

Liam snorted and stepped into the bathroom, which led to

a closet. In the center of the tile floor, Karina lay curled up on the rug. Liam crouched to feel for a pulse and felt a faint thump. Her face had been smashed by a fist, and the person wore a ring, judging by the cuts on her face. *Got yourself in over your head.*

"Karina." He gently shook her shoulder.

"We'll have to get another bus. She needs a hospital."

Liam nodded. "Karina, can you hear me?"

She moaned. Her lips parted, and she let out a puff of air.

"It's Liam. We're going to get you some medical help."

"He found out." She groaned, not turning those swollen eyes to look at him. One barely opened. "He found out."

"What did he find out, Karina?"

She blew out another breath.

Liam holstered his weapon, lifted her into his arms, and stood up. "Let's get you some help."

Her fingers curled into the top collar of his vest. "Lee?"

"Yeah, honey. It's me." He'd been watching out for her since he arrested her brother years ago and realized the two girls needed far better care than their brother had been giving them. He'd kept tabs. Made sure the foster care homes they ended up in treated them well. "Everything's going to be fine."

"He took her. Raphi." Karina let out a breath that tickled his neck. "He took your friend."

What had Karina been thinking, staying here? After Raphi had her kidnapped from her house, practically scaring the life out of her, she made some kind of deal? Tried to use her femininity to keep herself safe? He needed to sit her down and get her to talk so he could find out, but that would have to come after tonight was over.

He carried her downstairs where Gage and Blake stood in

the foyer. "Anything?" There were still spots upstairs to search if they were going to finish this.

Gage frowned. "Get her outside. The firefighters can treat her while an ambulance gets here."

Liam took Karina outside.

The firefighter met him on the lawn. "This is the woman you were looking for?"

"No, but she needs your help." Liam pressed his lips together.

"We've got her." He called for an ambulance on his radio.

Liam needed to get on the search. There were now three women from his life missing.

Karina grabbed his hand. Liam had to lean down to listen to her. "He's at Hurst—" Her body jerked, and she started to cough. Blood wet her lips. "Raphi."

"Does he have Roxie and the others?"

Her grip on his hand started to ease off. She was going to pass out. "He has everything."

THIRTY-SIX

One guy opened the door at the end of the long hallway by touching a key card to a square black panel on the wall beside the handle. A green light blinked on. He pushed down the handle, and Roxie got a look into the room. *Finally.*

Olivia and Destiny sat on the floor inside the empty room.

The man at the door held a gun where they could see it while the one behind her jabbed the nose of a pistol into her back. If only she could grab it with her hands, which they'd secured behind her with plastic ties.

Roxie clenched her back teeth and breathed slowly. All the air had to enter her body through her nostrils since they'd placed a thick piece of tape over her mouth. Wide as her eyes, most likely. She probably looked terrified, which would play in her favor if she worked it right.

She whimpered. That was good, it sounded really scared.

Sure, she might be outnumbered, but life constantly lay on a blade edge from death. The tipping point was what counted, and all she had to do was push it in her favor.

The man at the door snickered. These guys were the cops

who had shown up at the accountant's mom's house. Dirty cops.

They'd trussed her up and brought her to Hurstwhile before she could step one foot inside the house. Right after that SUV exploded and killed everyone inside.

Tears slid down her cheeks.

The guy at the door touched her hip. He'd touched more than that when he rid her of her weapons, close up in the back seat of the car. She'd managed to give him that bruise on his cheek with her knee, but there was little satisfaction in it.

She felt a hand on her behind and heard him say, "I get what he sees in you. He's got decent taste."

The door slammed shut behind her. Roxie flinched. Her nose started to run.

Destiny scrambled to her feet, her hands bound in front of her. Roxie frowned. Her friend said, "Let me get that tape off."

She stood still while Destiny worked the tape off for her. When it was gone, Roxie hissed out a breath. Felt like her lip was bleeding. Her hair hung all wispy around her face. Hands bound behind her back.

Olivia had her hands bound in front of her, but her wrists were so close together there was no way she'd be able to snap them free. It took force—and a gap between the hands—the older woman might not have.

There was no way Roxie could get out of hers.

The older woman dug awkwardly in her pocket and pulled out a bundled-up tissue. She winced. "It's not new, but it's better than nothing."

Roxie crouched beside her so they faced each other, and Liam's mom wiped her nose. "Sorry, Olivia."

"Honey, there's nothing to apologize for. This isn't your doing."

She couldn't form the words, too worried she would throw up if she talked. They'd even taken the GPS necklace. Things had not gone according to plan.

Roxie shifted to her back and worked her body and then her legs through her bound arms, bringing her hands in front of her. A lot harder than it looked. Though, from Olivia and Destiny's expressions, they'd considered it touch and go.

She sat up and crossed her legs. Everything swam around her, and she pressed the back of her hand to her mouth, hissing out a breath. "Oof."

"Yeah, please don't hurl, honey," Olivia said. She looked rumpled, but not like she'd been hurt. Just traumatized. "I'm a sympathy puker."

Roxie whimpered again. It was supposed to be a laugh, but there was no humor in this situation. "Tell me what's happened since you got here." The only thing she had the energy to do was lie back and stretch out her hip flexors. She needed to be the strong one with these two civilians, so she bent her arms and tucked her bound hands behind her back so she could prop her head on them.

Olivia blinked at the change in her demeanor.

Roxie said, "Catch me up."

Destiny stared at her like she'd grown a second head. "We're at Hurstwhile." She frowned. "The therapy center on the hill with the big flag outside."

Roxie nodded. "I saw that when we drove around to the garage."

"Me, too," Olivia said.

"Did those two guys take both of you?"

Olivia nodded, but Destiny said, "It was two guys who spoke Russian that got me." Her voice broke. "They hurt Conrad."

Roxie nudged her friend with her knee since it was closest. "We found him. He's at the hospital. He was talking to Liam."

"And Bob?"

Roxie glanced at Olivia and nodded. "Liam called you, and he picked up, said what'd happened."

Relief washed over Olivia's face, and she blew out a breath through pursed lips. "He's alive."

Roxie did the knee nudge in the other direction, since she was essentially lying between them. She was also facing away from the door. But it wouldn't take long for her to flip around and stand. Just as soon as someone came in.

She would stand between these two women and whoever entered.

No matter their intention.

It was what she knew Liam would ask of her. Not only that, but it was the person Roxie wanted to be. Whether she and Liam were a thing or not, she would stand up for the people she cared about. "I don't suppose the two of you have been praying."

"Only since we got here," Olivia said.

Destiny nodded. "Haven't stopped."

"Good. You can help me." She sucked in air and blew it out, still not entirely comfortable with admitting weakness. "I don't really know how to do it, but I know we need to." She clenched her abdominals and sat up. "Liam told me to trust God. He probably meant no matter what, not just...what we were talking about."

Olivia's brows rose. "And what would that be, dear?"

The woman was the picture of innocence. Given she was also the mom of three boys, she was probably far wiser than that. "I'm sure you can guess."

Olivia reached over and patted Roxie's knee. "Don't agree too easily. Make him work for it."

Roxie stared at her.

Destiny snorted, then clapped her bound hands over her mouth. "How are we going to get out of here?"

Roxie turned around far enough to see the back of the door. No handle on this side. "Have they said anything to you?"

"No." Olivia sounded small. Scared.

Roxie held her hand. "Destiny?" When her friend laid her hand on the bundle of Roxie and Olivia's, Roxie said, "Someone start us off praying. I'll learn as we go."

She closed her eyes and listened, absorbing the cadence of the words. They spoke with ease. A warmth and familiarity in their prayers that said it came natural now, like conversation with a loved one. As Olivia prayed, Destiny leaned forward and touched her shoulder with Roxie's, so they sat there in a kind of hug. Roxie leaned her head down onto her friend's, soaking up the nearness. Knowing God had made it so none of them were alone in this.

Help us.

She'd started to fall asleep sitting up when the door opened. It wasn't graceful or athletic, but she scrambled around. She didn't get up, just sat in front of the other two, tucking them behind her.

The first cop pointed at her. "That one."

Two men she would not want to meet in a dark alley grabbed her elbows and hauled her to her feet. She didn't look back at the others. She tuned out their cries and pleading. *Help us, Lord.* She had nothing else. No way out. No weapons. No backup. No team. No gear. No help. So much for the tracker and the plan.

Now it was just God.

If God was powerful enough to make the world, to come back from the dead, and to exchange all that was inside her for the peace she felt right now, then He could be all that in this situation as well. Everything she needed.

The two men walked her down the hall. Her hands had started to go numb. Not a good sign. At least her legs didn't give out. No need to find out how it would feel to be dragged —or whatever they would do to get her moving.

One guy said something to the other in Russian. Obolensky's men, though she hadn't seen Raphi himself.

They walked her all the way to the lobby where a lone man stood waiting.

When he turned, she couldn't hold back the gasp at seeing him here. They were giving her to him. *Mark.* "Hello, Brad." The words cracked, sounding hollow to her.

He grinned. "I guess you figured it out."

She swallowed back the vomit.

Brad addressed the two men next, "Tell Raphi he's clear. He doesn't owe me anymore."

THIRTY-SEVEN

The first shot came from Gage's gun. SWAT had the front and Vanguard had the other doors covered. Glass shattered, spraying the tile lobby of the Hurstwhile Center. Shots came at them from inside, and they fanned out to take shelter.

Liam bent a knee and held his rifle up. He squeezed off two shots, everything in him coalescing. Usually, all thought fled from his mind and instinct took over. This time, he kept hold of a single thought: *God, lead us.*

No way would he go into this without the cover of God's help through prayer. He could accomplish a whole lot on his own, but even Jesus said He could do nothing without the Father—so why discount God's help? He was still figuring out where his skill ended and God's work began, but he wouldn't take a step without a prayer on his lips tonight.

"Going," Jasper called out. A second later, he started moving. Blake did the same to his right, about six feet away. Firing as they moved.

Liam covered them, emerging from where he crouched and heading inside, along with the others.

Gage was pinned down behind the lobby desk.

Liam squeezed off a shot that allowed Gage to take a breath, get his feet under him, and get moving with them. "All that time behind a desk," Liam quipped. "Making you soft."

His lieutenant grunted. "I can still beat you in the training house."

Yes, he probably could. Liam chuckled. Then he spotted a guy heading for them. "Three!"

Jasper took the guy out.

Liam stepped over the man in the hall and recognized the face. "He's one of Raphi's guys."

"You think he's here?" Blake asked, his tone dark in a way that wasn't going to be good for Raphi if they found him.

"Steady." Liam said it like an order, even though Gage was the senior cop right now. He needed them to hold it together until they found the three women. His stomach clenched. Roxie had been taken from the house. A Vanguard operative was dead.

Peter had taken lead of the team on the far side of the building. Probably, it was as much about the fact Bob was in the hospital being treated as it was about his friend being missing. The kid cared a whole lot, and he was strong enough to back that up with the skills he'd accrued.

Good thing Liam wasn't on his bad side and that Vanguard was backing them up now. There were plenty of good cops, but the dirty ones—or whoever had paid the dispatcher to respond the way they had—soured him on calling for help. He'd use the police band in future, so no one could tell him his badge number didn't exist.

Clare was currently in a meeting with Russ Franklin and the FBI. They would get the particulars sorted out, but Liam didn't care about that when there were people here to be saved.

His mom. His best friend's sister. His Roxie.

God, go before us.

They cleared most of the ground floor. Vanguard headed upstairs, and they took the last hallway. Patient rooms. Treatment areas that should be full of residents, but each room was empty of occupants and furniture.

"Last door." Jasper started walking faster.

The entire hallway was a funnel that could spell their deaths if there were gunmen in the room. They hugged the walls and stacked up to hit the door.

Blake shifted Jasper out of the way and kicked it open himself.

They swept it, but Liam heard his mom cry out before Jasper and Blake were done looking in the corners and behind the door.

Blake cut his sister's hands free, and she launched at him, crying out. He held on to her.

Jasper cut Liam's mom free, but Liam was right there. "You okay?"

"Ready to get out of here." She smiled, but it was wobbly. She held her hands out so they could assist her to her feet. "Did you find Roxie?"

Liam hugged his mom, keeping her out of the way of all the pouches and weapons on his belt and attached to his vest. He rubbed up and down her back. "Conrad isn't awake, but they said he's stable."

She let out a breath.

"Bob is being treated, but the last I heard he's awake and making sense."

She squeezed him with the arms that had held him when he was little, when he cried or was sick. Now he got to hold her.

Liam needed to ask her for information now. "Now tell

me what that was about Roxie?"

Where was she?

He wanted to kick another door down. Find her.

Was she in the building, here somewhere?

His mom shifted and looked up at him. Rumpled but still very determined to survive. She wasn't the kind of woman who would back down, which was why it shouldn't have surprised him that she'd hired Vanguard. Even though it had come to this, she probably didn't regret her choice for a second.

The cost was high, but she'd saved more lives than what had been lost.

Tears filled her eyes now. "They took her. Two of the Russians, I think. They didn't look like those cops."

Liam turned to Gage. "We need to find those officers."

The lieutenant moved away down the hall and got on his radio. They were connected to the Vanguard radio frequency, and he could hear chatter through one earpiece but had been ignoring it. Sounded like they found someone upstairs, a man they'd detained.

Jasper said, "I'll get your mom taken care of."

Liam nodded but didn't move. He tried to go, but it was like his feet were stuck where they were. Was Roxie going to be dead by the time he got to her? After what he'd gained back with her in his life, he couldn't let her go all over again.

Until he found her, there was still hope. As soon as he did, the outcome would be final.

"Go, honey." Mom touched his cheek. "You need to find her before the little bit of faith she has falters."

What did that mean?

"She prayed with us."

Really? His brows rose. "She believes?"

"Find her. She needs you."

Liam hugged his mom again and kissed her forehead. "Love you."

"Yeah, yeah. I'm the best." She chuckled and shoved him toward the door. "Go find your girl."

Liam glanced at Destiny to make sure she was all right, then he went with Gage. They took the stairs to the floor above and found Peter standing above a guy rolled over onto his face. "Who is it? One of those cops?"

Peter shook his head. "They didn't make it."

They hauled the man to his feet, and Liam spotted the deadly look on Peter's face. They had him back behind them, but all the Vanguard people looked like they were about to tear the guy's head off. One of their people had been killed tonight and three were in the hospital—Bob and the two from the SUV bombing.

A bombing.

Liam looked at the man they'd stood up. "Raphi." He got into the guy's face. "Did you hire Brad Mills to plant that bomb that killed your uncle, Matvei?"

Raphi sneered. "Took you long enough to figure it out."

"Roxie wasn't downstairs." He grabbed two handfuls of Raphi's shirt. "Where is she?"

Raphi started to laugh.

Liam turned him and shoved him against the wall, pinning his hands behind his back. "Where is she?"

"I paid a debt." The Russian looked down his nose at everyone gathered, even though he did not have the upper hand right now.

"I'm surprised you owe anyone anything, but things haven't been going according to plan here, right? That's why you needed help from that guy in jail."

"Now I owe for that as well, but business will start up again." Raphi's jaw flexed.

"No, it won't," Liam said. "Because you're *done*."

He chuckled. "But so are you. Which means it wasn't a total loss."

"Where is she?"

"How should I know?"

Liam pulled him away from the wall, then slammed him against it again. *"Where is she?"* The words echoed in the hallway.

A note of fear flashed in Raphi's gaze. "I gave her to him. Payment for services rendered."

"Who?" Liam already knew, though. And every cell in his body wanted to blow but he reined in his anger.

"Brad Mills."

Gage tapped him on the shoulder. "Step back, Sergeant."

No. Liam planned to choke the life out of Raphi until he spilled Roxie's actual location. Could he really come this far only to lose her now? His heart had suffered plenty without her in his life. Thinking she'd chosen someone else when it was Mark's hateful words that had cut deep. If he'd spoken to her, he might have recognized the situation she'd been in and done what he could to save her.

They both knew it.

Perhaps it would be one of the biggest regrets they carried with them for the rest of their lives, the time they'd missed out on. But if he had saved her then, she might not be in this place where she could get into a relationship. She seemed at least closer to being ready for a relationship now.

He forced his fingers to let go of Raphi's shirt and backed off, replaced right away by Gage. The guy knew exactly how he felt. Gage and Clare had been through plenty before they finally settled into their relationship. And quickly got married. Though, with the lives they both lived, things would never be completely peaceful, would they?

"I need to know where she is." Gage's tone was one Liam had never heard.

Liam leaned his shoulder against the wall and closed his eyes. He prayed in a way he never had before. *Don't let him hurt her.* Begging felt odd, but there were plenty of verses that talked about asking God for things—and continuing to ask. Being persistent to the point God couldn't help but take notice, figuratively speaking.

Psalms of request to God rolled through his mind, and he found himself whispering them. Peter's hand squeezed his shoulder. Someone else moved.

He heard the muffled thud of a fist hitting center mass through clothes.

"Raphi, you know where he is." Gage stood over the Russian, who glared up at him from the floor.

Liam would have killed him by now, and then they would have no shot at getting this information from him.

"Where would he take her?"

When Raphi said nothing, Gage shifted his stance. To anyone watching, it would look like the lieutenant was about to kick his stomach. Of course, his commanding officer would never do that to a man on the ground, not even in the worst of situations.

All they needed was for Raphi to believe he would.

Gage shifted his weight. "Where?"

"All right." Raphi flinched. "He has a cabin. A place off the grid. I don't know where it is."

Liam nearly threw up right then.

Gage said, "Start telling me what you *do* know about it."

Peter had his phone out and put it to his ear. "A cabin off the grid, Sie." He paused, then said into the phone, "Brad Mills. Mark Mills." Another pause, then, "Find it."

THIRTY-EIGHT

The car jerked to a stop like he'd slammed on the brakes. Roxie moaned from her spot in the trunk, her stomach roiling in a way that didn't spell anything good. She might not have eaten much recently, but it didn't seem to matter when bile rose in her throat anyway.

She heard his door slam. Then footsteps in gravel, which matched what she'd heard when they'd pulled off the steady rumble of the blacktop.

The trunk lid lifted.

She braced, flinching so hard it shot pain through her. He'd hit her with a stun gun on her front, hitting her collar bone. She hadn't been able to hold back the cry, and the fact it still hurt even after that drive was bad news.

"Get out."

She opened her mouth to tell him no, just on principle, but didn't think that would go well for her. "Might take me a minute, *Brad*." She kept a tone in her voice like, *Yeah, I know exactly who you are, and you don't scare me anymore, Mark.* Hopefully, pretending would cause her to believe it at least a little bit. Some of that "fake it till you make it" with some more hope—that she'd get rescued or manage to escape before she found out if it worked or not.

"You're not going to call me that. Because I'm Mark."

Yeah, duh.

Did he want to have a discussion about what was true and what wasn't? Another thing that probably wouldn't go well for her. What would he do to punish her if she did or said something he didn't like?

This guy needed a little truth, but what about the consequences? Roxie managed to push herself to sitting in the trunk, her hands still bound in front. The prayer so strong it nearly escaped her lips aloud. *How about a rescue? I don't know how it works to ask for help other than to just ask.*

This felt a whole lot different than it had with Mark.

Maybe because *she* was different.

Is that Your doing? Maybe God had done this in her, bringing her to a point where she could face this man with strength and peace in her heart.

Roxie sat on the edge of the trunk and swung her legs over.

He touched the stun gun to her leg. Her entire body spasmed, and she hit the ground, her face in the dirt. *Breathe.* She coughed. Pain exploded in her chest. She started to count silently, tuning out the world and Brad, and focusing the way she'd learned.

Something.

She was lying on something. *No.* She refused to be incapacitated in front of him.

Roxie pushed off the ground, got her feet under her, and stood. She turned to face him, chin up. Head high. All that. Never mind that she could barely breathe. "So here we are." Her voice didn't sound solid, but it was what it was.

He studied her, unsure for a second.

"What do you want, Brad?" Maybe if she got him talking, she could drag this out until help came. Or until she figured out how to escape him.

All around them was nothing but trees. The full moon above shone bright enough that she could see plenty even without another light. Giant towering trunks and pine needles were strewn over the ground from trees that had been growing here for decades. In the center of a tiny clearing, there was a cabin, old and run-down. As if it had been here for the same amount of time.

She'd have cleared away more trees in case a storm blew one down and flattened the house. Still, it seemed to have worked since the structure was still standing where it should be.

"I'm Mark." He came toward her, lifting that stun gun.

She backed up, stumbling slightly on the uneven dirt. Pain. "Sure, *Brad*. You're Mark? Funny, because I saw him burn to death. All that flickering heat melting his skin."

His hand whipped out, and he cuffed her across the face with the back of his hand that was holding the stun gun.

She reacted only in her mind. *Ouch*. That had hurt a whole lot. But she managed to straighten, pushing aside everything in a way that wasn't going to last long. "The best part was the smell."

He came at her.

Roxie kicked her leg out, smashing it down on his leg from an angle. The world spun around her. *Breathe*.

His leg gave out, and he went down on one knee. "You murdered him!"

He launched at her, but she started to run before her mind even processed what the sudden rush of movement meant.

Instinct and self-preservation. *And You.*

She made it two steps. Then, he grabbed her leg, and she hit the ground again. Far too slow. Too weak. Too much of nothing, the way Mark had said she was. Over and over, until she'd believed it.

Roxie pushed up. More pain.

He was on her then. Grasping. Hitting.

Flashes of pain sparked in her side, gone as fast as they came. She fought for air, his weight cutting off her ability to take a full breath. *God.*

She tried to push up. That didn't work. Tried to use her legs, then her bound hands. Her feet. None of it could get his weight off her.

The same way Mark had beat her. At the end, when it became the worst of all.

She screamed as loudly as she could, expelling all the fear and those tormenting memories that haunted her nightmares. Now, she was living it once again, and there was nothing she could do.

Brad started to laugh. She twisted as much as she could, throwing her full force into her movement, and her elbow contacted something.

Then his weight was gone.

Roxie squeezed her eyes shut and breathed. The eye of the storm, not the end of it. Just a calm in the center while every terrifying thing in her mind swirled around her about to strike.

She rolled to her back, feeling bare skin against the grass where her shirt had ridden up at the small of her back. Pain lanced through every muscle, every limb, everywhere. She coughed. Her whole body spasmed, trying to take in enough air. She gasped, then held her breath at the top. Tried to slow her heart rate, control her breathing.

Help is coming.

She had to believe it. Before with Mark, she'd had no hope. Now, she had all the hope available to her from God. Coworkers who cared about her. A friend who loved her and who she prayed was all right even now. She had a man who probably felt about her the way she felt about him.

Liam.

She wanted to see him. To hang on to him with every bit of strength she had left so she could soak up some of his. And he would let her rely on him. She would be safe, allowing him to fight for her, in a way she had never been safe. Not once in her life.

Brad tossed the stun gun on the grass, too far away for her to reach. He pulled a pistol from the back of his waistband. "I was going to get you into the house, take my time, and carve you up. Nice and slow." He spat on the grass. "You're not even worth it."

Roxie didn't move. She just lay there on the grass, staring up at him. Would her next breath be her last?

"You can die here in the dirt for all I care." He aimed the pistol at her.

Roxie squeezed her eyes shut.

A gunshot cracked through the quiet of the night. She flinched, bracing for the pain that never came. Something landed on her foot, bending it to the side. She looked and saw Brad lying in the dirt, dead eyes staring at her. Mark's eyes.

She scrambled back on her elbows. Freeing herself from the weight of him.

Sound and sight washed around her, the world swirling with movement. People. Flashlights. The smell of gunpowder and sweat.

She tried to move but found herself flat on her back again. Staring up at the full moon. Trying to get air.

Someone pressed cold fingers to her neck. "Roxie!"

Liam's face floated into view. White spots sparked at the edges of her vision like fireworks going off.

She tried to breathe. "Liam." Barely any sound came out of her mouth.

A dog licked her face. He shoved it away. "Not now, puppy."

"Breathe, Roxie. You need to breathe." He turned to look at someone else. "Medic!"

Was he hurt? They needed help! Her thoughts swam around her like the ocean at night. "*God.*"

Someone touched the sides of her face. Kissed her forehead. Her cheeks. Her lips. "I love you." She savored the warmth of the words whispered in her ear.

And then everything went black.

THIRTY-NINE

Conrad lay on the hospital bed. Liam eased the door all the way open but didn't go in. He'd showered and put on fresh clothes, hit a drive-through for a coffee and a breakfast burrito, and then come right back to the hospital.

Conrad's wife sat at the foot of the bed, and his girls were lying down on either side while he read them a story.

Liam listened for a moment. The girls were drifting off to sleep, the only reason why they hadn't spotted their favorite uncle at the door. He smiled, loving the way their eyelashes fluttered.

Conrad looked from his wife to Liam and lifted his chin.

Liam waved.

Conrad mouthed, *You good?*

He nodded, then mouthed back, *She's in surgery.* Conrad's wife had checked in with their mom hours ago and got the skinny on Destiny's minor injuries, but Liam hadn't been able to update his brother on Roxie before he headed home for thirty minutes just so he didn't inconvenience anyone.

Liam eased out and closed the door behind him. He was holding it together until Roxie got out of surgery and he got word that she was all right. Until then, he was avoiding the people he worked with. Holding his phone instead of putting it in his pocket, praying every second that it would ring and he'd find out she was out of surgery. Awake.

He used the empty stairs rather than the elevator, just to avoid people. At the door to the fourth floor, he grabbed the handle and stopped. Took a long breath, alone.

God, don't let her die.

It had taken far too much time to find her. Raphi had only given them a rough area where he thought the cabin might be. Peter and Simon had found records of property in the area owned by Mark's wife's family. They'd managed to find the place in the dense woods. A cabin so old it was no longer on any maps. Only one road in and out, which was washed out or overgrown in places.

They'd found her just in time.

Barely.

She'd been on the ground and hadn't gotten up. Brad had been about to shoot her dead when Liam squeezed off a shot and dropped the guy. No guilt. Her problems were over, and it was he that had put an end to all of it.

When she woke up from surgery, she would have nothing to worry about.

Not *if* she woke up, but *when.*

He said another prayer, refusing to lose hope, and headed for his mom's room. Liam waited for her to answer his knock and then stepped in. She lay in the bed reading a magazine. She had a bandage on one wrist but was otherwise uninjured.

"Hey." He went over and kissed her forehead. "How are you feeling?"

She folded the magazine closed and shot him a look. "Me? Really? How are you, kiddo?"

Liam sat on the side of the bed, facing the wall. She touched his elbow. He couldn't speak for a few minutes.

"You didn't tell me how she is."

All he'd said before he left was that Roxie was in surgery, kind of like the nothing update he'd just given Conrad so his brother wouldn't needlessly worry. "She'll be okay."

"Liam Sheamus O'Connell, you tell your mother the truth right now."

He gritted his teeth. "Her lung was punctured. Brad threw her on the ground and there was a rock that penetrated her chest." He had to swallow to give himself a second so he could keep going. "Her chest filled with air and collapsed her lung from the weight of it. One of the Vanguard guys—"

His mom didn't want all the gory details of a pocketknife, a plastic tube from a ballpoint pen, and the sound of air escaping Roxie's chest. At least she'd started to breathe again thanks to a guy with medical training. Her heart rate had come back up, and they'd stabilized her before Life Flight showed up.

It was the only thing that kept him going while watching them tape the pen in place and carry her to a clearing so the local Life Flight helicopter could land.

"God holds her in His hands." His mom squeezed his arm again. "You either believe that or you don't. It's not about whether she lives or how she fares through surgery. He's either your good God or He isn't."

"I know." Faith wasn't contingent on whether God did what he wanted or not. "It's like Dad all over again." He winced and looked at her, the burn of tears in his eyes. "Roxie was there. When I found out Dad had been killed in the line of duty. She held on to me."

"And you want the chance to hold on to her now."

Liam nodded, not able to reply out loud.

"Every day without your father is worth it for the ones we had together. The ones I can only cherish in my memories."

Liam sniffed. "I miss him."

"He loved you so much. He would be so proud of you."

Liam puffed a breath through his lips. "You're the one who exposed what happened. Gage told me that Lieutenant Turnbull was arrested. He lied about how Dad died. He's the one who killed him, in the confusion. He used the homeless man's gun to shoot his partner in the back."

Eventually, Liam would go see the man, to have the satisfaction of seeing his father's killer behind bars. But when he did, would he be able to keep himself from killing that man?

He pushed out a long breath and squeezed the bridge of his nose.

"I love you, honey."

"I know, Mom."

"You need to convince that girl to marry you. Then I'll be able to worry about you a little less because I'll know you're in good hands. Just like Conrad with his sweet Amanda."

Liam leaned over and kissed her forehead again. "Love you, too."

"And go see Rory. I need to know he's all right, and I just don't want to go to Alaska. Unless it's on a cruise."

He chuckled.

The door opened, and he heard a man say, "Whoops, sorry."

Liam twisted, which felt great. *Liar.* Bob Davis stood at the door, a bandage around his head.

"Should you be out of bed?" Liam asked.

Bob waved a hand. "I feel fine."

Liam got up. "Come in. I was just about to go hassle the nurses for an update."

Bob's cheeks pinked.

Liam looked at his mom. "Stay out of trouble."

She chuckled. "No promises."

And no need for him to get involved with her love life. But if she were ever to date again—or get remarried—the fact it was a guy he respected didn't hurt. Even though Bob had been convicted as a corrupt cop, he'd done his time and now worked a job that helped make the world better by bringing justice where none had been found.

Like helping his mom learn the truth about her husband's death.

He spotted a crowd of Vanguard employees in the waiting area outside of surgery. Clare and Gage saw him right away, stood, and came over.

Gage held out his hand, and they hugged. Clare kissed his cheek.

"Any word?"

Gage said, "Not yet. But Jasper told me Raphi has been booked. His business is decimated. Karina is telling the prosecutor everything. And the feds are descending on Hurstwhile. Everything they're into is going to be exposed. Internal Affairs will comb through the lives of the two officers killed at the center. No one wants dirty cops, so it's up to the department to figure out what made them go bad."

"It's over?" Everything he'd been working at for years was finally done. Not just that, but his father's memory was finally at peace. There was no longer any suspicion that his father had been dirty.

And Roxie never had to be afraid.

Clare nodded, then Gage.

Clare said, "And when Roxie is back on her feet, I've got a

meeting penciled in. I'd like to run something by you. An idea for a new position. Something you two can do together."

Liam frowned. "Does it involve me retiring from the Benson PD?"

Clare shrugged one shoulder. "Unlikely, but it's possible if that's what you want."

He scratched his chin, his mind reeling. They didn't even know if Roxie was alive, and Clare was making plans for the future. What was taking the surgery so long? Surely, they should know the outcome by now.

Gage clapped a hand on his shoulder. "It'll keep until Roxie is ready to come with you to the meeting."

Before Liam could say anything more, a doctor opened the door. "Is there a Liam O'Connell here?"

He twisted around and lifted two fingers. "Me."

"Ms. Helton is out of surgery." The doctor looked flushed and exhausted but pleased. "She's awake and asking for you."

EPILOGUE

T HREE WEEKS LATER

Roxie twisted around to get out of the car, barely managing to bite back the groan.

Liam strode to the back of the SUV he'd bought to replace his mangled truck. "You were supposed to wait for me to help you."

She grunted and reached for his arm, her teeth gritted. "Everything's fine."

He stared at her, managing to keep a straight face. "I could always carry you."

"I'll shoot you before you pick me up."

He grinned. "Some women like to be carried."

If he tried that any day other than their wedding night, he would find out how she felt about it.

Liam wound her arm in his. "Shall we?"

She pressed her lips together. Why was the front door of

Vanguard so far away? They hadn't parked that far from the entrance. She was sweating by the time they stepped onto the elevator.

"Good?"

"I want to know what this summons is about." She hadn't returned to work since she left the hospital nine days ago. All she'd done was lay on the couch and watch terrible TV, hang out with Destiny—and her sisters. The girls showed up at random times because "they were bored," as if Roxie didn't know it was because Destiny didn't want her left alone.

Then when the group wasn't working, she got visits from Jasper—who insisted on looking longingly at Destiny when she wasn't looking—and Blake, Gage and Clare, Conrad and his wife, but without the kids, and Olivia.

And Liam.

She didn't think she'd been alone since she'd been alone with Brad. Thinking about him made Roxie lean her head against Liam's wide bicep. "It's quiet in here."

"Good thing it'll be at the right floor soon."

"I like the—"

The elevator doors slid open to dead silence and a room full of people. Lena stood right in front of the doors, a box and her purse and coat in her hands. They stepped off the elevator, and she stepped onto it.

The doors slid closed.

Roxie glanced at the shut elevator.

Then, the room erupted into noise. "Roxie!" Cheering. Clapping. A room full of smiling faces in every corner of the place, all staring at her and Liam while her face flamed.

"Like you all haven't seen me since the hospital."

Peter strode over. "Every day is a miracle. You didn't know that?"

Liam let go of her, and Peter gave her an easy hug. He

knew how much her chest still hurt. Felt like an elephant had sat on it, if she was honest. "Yeah, yeah. Okay." She shoved, and he let her go. "Calm down, everyone."

"No way." Simon grinned. "There's cake in the break room."

She shook her head, smiling. "Well, then. If there's cake. I can hardly say no."

Simon nodded. "Exactly."

Peter shook Liam's hand. "They're waiting for you in Clare's office."

So this was it.

She held his hand and managed to snag Bob for a hug around his paper plate of more frosting than cake. "Good to see you."

"Mmm." He lifted his brows.

What was that about? She didn't have time to ask before Liam tugged her on.

The door to Clare's office was open. And the receptionist's desk was clear.

"Did you just fire your assistant?" They strode into the office, and Roxie spotted the two federal agents—and their K-9. "Hi, honey." She crouched, and the dog came over to sniff her. Roxie rubbed her shoulders first, then all the way down her sides while the dog sniffed at her face. "Hello, gorgeous."

The dark-haired female agent—Dakota—chuckled. "She has that effect on quality people."

Liam shook both their hands, then turned to her and helped her get upright.

Once Roxie stood, she looked at Clare. "Did you fire Lena?"

"Yes." Clare said nothing else. *Okay, then.* "These agents requested a meeting with the two of you." She didn't look entirely happy.

Kind of like Liam in the last few weeks, trying to figure out what position to take. He'd told her he enjoyed his job—the way it had been with SWAT. Roxie had been encouraging him that whatever he decided should be what he wanted and not feel like settling. But was that even right? Maybe he should just take what he could get and learn to be content.

Still, there was so much about her life now that felt like pure magic. The kind that meant God—and only He—could have brought her here.

Dakota stepped toward them while her husband and partner on the taskforce hung back, using hand signals to have his dog sit. "Liam. Roxie. You know I run the Northwest Counter-Terrorism Taskforce already. Well, we're a unique team made up of agents and officers from different agencies and even a few civilians. What started as an exercise in cooperation between police and federal agencies has developed into a family. It's unique work, and we go all over the northwest and into Alaska."

Roxie looked at Liam, whose eyes had flared. He wanted to visit his brother.

Dakota said, "You're welcome to come to Seattle. See the office we work out of and the kind of things we do. I have open slots, and the bottom line is that I'd like the two of you to fill them." She glanced at Roxie. "You're not a cop, but like I said, we have civilian positions. Liam, we would like to add a police sergeant to our team. Your department highly recommends you, although I was warned that I'd be stealing you from them and they might begrudge me that *forever*." She smiled.

Roxie reached over and squeezed Liam's hand.

Dakota said, "It would be a reassignment for you, Sergeant O'Connell. But we'd be lucky to have you, by the sound of it."

Roxie sniffed back tears. Clare did not look happy at the prospect. Because she didn't want to lose them.

Clare waved a hand. "Ignore me. Hormones."

Roxie's brows rose. Her friend was pregnant? Liam glanced at her—likely since she'd squeezed his hand. She glanced at him and whispered, "Clare and Gage are having a baby."

Dakota's eyes widened.

Behind her, Josh flushed red and grinned. "What a happy coincidence. Us, too."

Liam chuckled and tugged Roxie closer to his side. She grinned, leaning her head against his arm for a second. Then she looked up at him. "What do you say? Want to go pay a taskforce a visit about two open positions?"

She recognized that light in his eyes. He smiled at her and nodded, then looked at Dakota. "Yes, I'd like that. If Roxie is on board, then so am I."

There was a whole lot of handshaking—a few tears from Clare, who was apparently convinced they would leave and never come back—and they made plans to visit the next week.

An hour later, they were at Liam's, pulling into his garage. She was exhausted. "Your house?"

"I have to go to work in fifteen minutes." He looked at his watch. "That took longer than I thought. There's probably a big mess inside."

"Why would there—" She pushed open the door, which hurt a lot, and heard a high, sharp barking noise over the cooling of the engine. "What is that?"

He smiled. "Come on."

She went first, not wasting a single moment. In his living room, he'd pushed aside furniture and set up a wire enclosure. Inside, a slender, tiny puppy with dark brown hair and black patches stood up on all fours with its ears straight up.

"A Malinois?"

Liam winced. "That might've been a bad choice. They're not for the average dog owner."

"I've worked with a few." She sniffed. He'd bought her a dog.

"Mitchell said she should have a calmer temperament, but that also might be a misnomer. She *is* a Malinois."

Roxie had a feeling that might become a common phrase between them. "What is her name?"

Liam opened the enclosure, so the dog raced to him and put two front paws on his shins. He told her to sit, then petted her head as a reward.

Roxie sank onto the couch. The dog ran to her and repeated the front paws move. She said, "I want to pick her up."

"Don't let her rule the roost."

"Right." *Of course not.* She leaned forward far enough to pet the dog, who sniffed at her hands, smelling the taskforce dog, Neema, on her. "Hi, precious."

"You want to call her that?"

"What?" Roxie stared. "A dog like this doesn't get a cute name. She's fierce."

"Figure it out while I go to work, okay? Call me if you need help with her. Or if you need to take her out. Or if you need anything. Or—"

"I love you. Don't worry." She scratched the dog's face. "We'll be just fine, right?" This dog needed a name, pronto. "That's it." She grinned at Liam. "Her name is Pronto."

"Uh." He chuckled. "Okay."

She watched him switch out some gear for work, adding his badge and gun. He'd been given a job offer, effectively a chance to stretch his wings in a new role. It had altered his demeanor in a visible way—and maybe she also had something to do with that.

He came over, set a hand on the back of his couch, and leaned down to kiss her. "I love you, too."

"I know." He'd told her every day since she'd woken up from surgery.

"Anytime you want to marry me, I'm there."

He'd also told her that every day. "I know." She held his shirt collar. "Be safe tonight."

A familiar tang filled the air, then the sound of a trickle of liquid hitting his boot.

"Can you take the dog outside? Maybe try and get her to pee there instead of on my shoe?"

Roxie held her laughter in, amazed that didn't make him angry. Not that Liam never got mad. It was that he never took it out on her.

She said, "I'll clean the carpet as well. No worries. I've got this."

"You're sure?"

She nodded.

"I know you do." He straightened. "I didn't doubt you for a second."

ABOUT THE AUTHOR

Find out more about Lisa Phillips at her website, where you can check out her work with Sunrise Publishing and find Lisa on Social Media.
https://authorlisaphillips.com/about-the-author

If you loved this book, please consider sharing about it on social media. Or leave a review at your book retailer website, on Goodreads, or on Bookbub. Your review will help others find great books to entertain and encourage them! For a FREE novel from Lisa Phillips, scan the QR code below to connect to Lisa's newsletter and be the first to hear about sales, new books, and recommendations for your TBR pile.

facebook.com/authorlisaphillips
instagram.com/lisaphillipsbks
bookbub.com/authors/lisa-phillips

ALSO BY LISA PHILLIPS

Find out more about Benson First Responders on the series page:

https://authorlisaphillips.com/benson-first-responders

Benson First Responders is a continuation of Last Chance Downrange. Read the whole Last Chance Downrange series now!

Point of Impact

Hard Target

Hollow Point

Terminal Velocity

Audio Available from Podium Publishing

Find more stories based in Last Chance County at:
www.lastchancecounty.com

Other series by Lisa:

Brand of Justice (Thriller series)

Benson First Responders (Christian Romantic Suspense)

Last Chance Fire & Rescue (Sunrise Publishing)

Chevalier Protection Specialists

Last Chance County

Northwest Counter-Terrorism Taskforce

Double Down

WITSEC Town (Sanctuary)

And numerous other titles including several from

Love Inspired Suspense.

Find the complete list here:

https://authorlisaphillips.com/full-book-list